# Our Moon

by Jennifer L. Allen

## Our Moon

## Copyright © 2015 Jennifer L. Allen

Published: Jennifer L. Allen 2015

jenniferlallenauthor@gmail.com

Editor: Aimee Lukas
Cover Design: Pink Ink Designs

## Dedication

This book is dedicated to my husband.
Thank you for putting up with my crap.
Thank you for everything else.
I love you.

# Part One
## Ally

# Chapter One

"That's about it. Does anyone have any questions?" Dr. Moody asks as she finishes her spiel. Yep, that's right. A psychiatrist named Dr. Moody. It doesn't get much better than that, folks. Her appearance is much softer than her name, though, light brown hair with freckled skin and a slightly rounded middle. She has a very soothing, grandmotherly demeanor, quite the contradiction to her name.

I peer over at my two brothers, seated awkwardly across the coffee table from me and Dr. Moody. I stifle a laugh; they look about as uneasy as I feel. Trevor is leaning forward with his elbows resting on his knees, while one foot taps non-stop, causing his entire body to shake. Alex is slouching back in his seat, his legs stretched out in front of him, with the most confused expression on his face. Night and day, those two. I hope I'm not wearing my emotions so transparently.

I imagine the long list of my possible behaviors, which Dr. Moody just listed, read like the various side effects on one of those medication commercials I'd seen on the television in the common room: irritability, anxiety, disorientation, depression, and the list goes on. It's enough to make anyone twitch, I suppose. Especially when they're going to be living with someone with said side effects.

"I think we've got it all," my older brother, Trevor, says. I don't know him well, but from what I've made out during our many family sessions, he's the responsible, older brother. He's also really tall, like six-five tall. Might not seem like a big deal, but I'm only about five-two, so that's huge to me.

Alex is more easy-going. He's also my twin. We share the same blue eyes and sandy blonde hair. He's between Trevor and me in height, about six feet, I would guess. I only know Trevor's exact height because he caught me gazing up at him in absolute wonder once and told me. Trevor has referred to Alex and me as "double trouble" more than once over the past month. I'm interested to see if and how this twin dynamic between Alex and me will play out. I've often caught him looking at me as though he's trying to see inside of me. I can only imagine what losing his other half must have felt like, if what Trevor says about our bond is true.

Dr. Moody nods at Trevor and then looks at me. "Are you sure you're okay with this, Allyson? You know you're more than welcome to stay at our facility as long as you feel necessary. The last thing any of us wants is for you to feel pressured into doing something that makes you uncomfortable."

You see, just over a month before this little meeting, I woke up from a year-long coma. What's better than that? I have amnesia. The two men sitting across from me are perfect strangers, yet I've supposedly known them my whole life. I was in a car accident with my parents the night of my high school graduation. I ended up with a banged up head, and they ended up in the ground. I should be sad about this fact, and I guess a part of me is sad at the idea that my parents are dead, but I can't remember them to mourn them. That alone is a bit depressing. I'm not trying to be insensitive, I just don't know how to feel about it, so I honestly try not to think about it.

Even though I didn't die in the accident, I might as well have. I was in a coma for a year, just to wake up with no memory of who I am or who they are. Not only did my brothers lose their parents, but they practically lost their sister as well, first to the coma and then to her own head. In one of our earliest sessions, I once said that they would have been better off if I *had* died, and that resulted in a twenty-four hour suicide watch, and my brothers FREAKING out, so I don't dare voice those thoughts out loud anymore.

Don't get me wrong, I'm not suicidal. Yes, I'm sure many people who are suicidal may claim that they're not suicidal, but I'm really not. I've just had many moments where I've felt so lost and confused, like I don't know what to think or feel because I don't know what my former self would have thought or felt. Dr. Moody says it's not uncommon to be depressed and/or anxious when you have amnesia. Yay me! Looks like I have a lot to look forward to. She has also been a strong advocate of letting things happen naturally and not trying too hard to think about what the old Ally would do, the real Ally.

I've been in this rehab facility for about four weeks, regaining my motor skills through physical therapy and participating in various psychological therapies designed for individuals with amnesia. There are other people like me here, and it has actually been nice participating in the group therapies and having people to commiserate with. I've started to feel less lost and confused as I've participated in group. But today I'm going home.

To be honest, I am a little nervous about leaving. Not because I'm afraid of my brothers, because I'm not. I've actually grown quite fond of them during our time together at the rehab facility. I was introduced to them about a week after I woke from the coma. When I first woke up, I was extremely confused and disoriented, and then I became quite hysterical when I couldn't remember anything, even my own name. The doctors felt it was necessary for me to adjust to my situation a little bit before bringing them in. Something that, I later learned, broke their hearts. They wanted to be there for me, but they couldn't. There really was no easy way to handle it, but when they realized it was what was best for me, they forgave themselves for not being there.

It took a few days for me to calm down from my initial freak out, during which time there were lots of scans and tests. Apparently they always knew amnesia could be a factor due to my head injury, but there was no telling until I was awake. And there was also no telling if the problem would ever correct itself. On the sixth day, I was properly introduced to Trevor and Alex. We had an hour long session guided by Dr. Moody. I timidly asked questions about my life and they answered as simply as possible, as advised by Dr. Moody. She didn't want me to have information overload.

These sessions continued every other day for the rest of my stay, but after two weeks, and at Dr. Moody's recommendation, we added free visits. This meant that Trevor and Alex could come and visit with me as long as any of us wanted, as long as it was within visiting hours, without Dr. Moody or any of the other facility staff monitoring us. It was designed that way to make me comfortable with my brothers in a less structured environment. And it worked, I am comfortable with them.

The reason I'm nervous about leaving is because I have no idea what is waiting for me on the outside. I've been stuck in this little semi-microcosm, not having to deal with the real world at all, and all of a sudden, I will be in the great wide open. The wild, as far as I know. I know Trevor and Alex won't just throw me to the wolves or anything like that. I know that they will take good care of me. I know it. But I can't help but worry a little. I have to relearn how to be a productive member of society. Something no amount of therapy can prepare me for. Immersion is the only way to do it.

I give Dr. Moody a small smile. "Thank you, Dr. Moody. But I'm ready to go home." The half-truth is worth the ginormous grins on my brothers' faces. I can't help but smile wider at them. Things are definitely going to be interesting with these two.

"Okay, then, I'll go get your discharge paperwork ready. Why don't you have your brothers help get your room packed up, and we'll meet back up in the lobby?"

It doesn't take long to pack up my stuff as I don't have much to begin with, so the boys and I are out in the lobby in no time. After a bunch of signatures and more reassurances from Dr. Moody, we say goodbye, and I leave the only home I've ever known behind.

# Chapter Two

As Trevor turns his giant SUV into a quaint neighborhood, I can't help but be a little shocked. My two brothers, who are in a rock band (did I mention that?), live in suburbia. Like picket fence, 2.5 kids, golden retriever, American dream, suburbia.

"This is where you live?" I ask from the backseat, taking in the stone sign surrounded by colorful flowers that indicates we've now entered Pleasant Pointe.

"No," Trevor says, looking at me in the rear view mirror. "This is where *we* live."

I roll my eyes, "You know what I mean."

"Don't think we fit the mold of the rest of the residents of this fine neighborhood, baby sis?" Alex asks with a sarcastic smirk.

"You're like four minutes older than me," I grumble. He has used the "baby/little sis" line on me about thirty times in the past week alone, don't get me started on the count for the month. "It's just that you're in a rock band, right? You said you went on tour and all that. I just didn't imagine a couple of bachelor rock stars living here. That's all."

I look back out the window, taking in all the perfectly manicured lawns as we pass by, I swear one even has a "Yard of the Month" sign. There are kids riding bicycles and scooters, people walking dogs; it's a picturesque summer day.

"It's the house we grew up in," Trevor finally says.

And I instantly. Feel. Horrible.

I have zero emotional attachment to the house we grew up in, can't remember it, but they obviously do. I feel like I just crapped on one of their precious memories.

"I'm sorry; I didn't know." I look down at my hands, fidgeting in my lap. I have no idea what I'm doing, or what I'm going to do. See? This is me: entering the wild. With apparently no people skills whatsoever, especially empathy.

"It's all good, Al," Alex says in his usual carefree tone, instantly making me feel a little better. Maybe that's his twin power, relaxing me or something. "Your room is exactly the way it was when you left it. We didn't touch it. I mean, I guess the cleaning lady probably dusted and maybe put up dirty clothes and whatever other grimy shit you had in there. You were such a pig."

Trevor laughs at that. "Right, like you're one to talk. The only reason we had to hire Myra in the first place is because even you won't clean up after your pig ass."

I smile at their banter. This is what the past few weeks were like. Even if I can't relate and don't know exactly where I fit in, I feel comfortable with and am entirely amused by my brothers.

I look out the window again as Trevor slows the car and pulls into a driveway. The house ahead of us sparks no recognition in me. Dr. Moody stressed that I may never regain my memory, but I also heard her when she said that certain things, like objects that stimulate the senses such as scents or sounds, may bring things back. But the two story brick home with perfectly placed black shutters does nothing. Honestly, I'm more than a little disappointed.

Trevor parks, and we all get out. I stand beside the beast of a vehicle and stare up at the house, willing a memory to come. Are one of those windows mine? Did I learn how to ride my bike in this driveway? Take my first steps just inside the front door? Have my first kiss on the front porch? Have I even been kissed?

The emotions whirling through my head start to become too much and the anxiety Dr. Moody warned us all about begins to set in. My vision gets blurry, my hands start shaking and my breath is coming in pants. I lean back against the car and close my eyes.

*Deep breaths.*

*In.*

*Out.*

*In.*

*Out.*

A hand touches my shoulder; another presses against my back. *Safe. I feel safe.* I begin to relax.

"You got this, baby sis." It's Alex. He moves his hand from my back to my waist and tugs me into his side. Relaxation is definitely his twin power.

Trevor squeezes my shoulder and with a small smile tells me, "Take all the time you need."

I get my breathing under control and nod, "I'm okay. I'm ready."

With my brothers flanking me, extending their strength and comfort like a warm blanket around my shoulders, I make it into the house. The house is as modest on the inside as it is on the outside. But I can immediately tell this is a home, not just a house, and not a crash pad or a bachelor's paradise. But a home that was built with love. I can feel that.

We enter into a gorgeous foyer with dark wood stairs matching the floors straight in front of us. To the immediate left, there appears to be a small bathroom or closet, the door is closed so I can't tell, and beyond that is an elegant living room with cream carpets, attached to a formal dining room that looks to have marble floors. I suspect those rooms must have been our parents' touches because I can't see Trevor or Alex doing any kind of formal entertaining. The interior design seems a bit more mature as well. To the left of the stairs there is a walkway, through which I catch a glimpse of the kitchen, and I make a mental note to explore that later. To the right of the foyer, there's a television and game room with a gigantic TV, standard-size pool table, and some kind of arcade game. It's the only sign, so far, that a couple of bachelors live here.

"I'm going to get your bags from the car," Trevor says and walks back out the front door.

"Come on, I'll show you to your room," Alex takes my hand and leads me up the stairs. "We can do the tour later, figure you'll want to get settled in first," he explains. I nod and follow him up the stairs.

I silently take in the framed photographs lining the staircase. It looks to be a timeline of our lives, starting with our parents' wedding and ending with what appears to be my prom, with various baby, childhood and adolescent milestones in between. I saw pictures like these in the albums the guys brought to the facility during our sessions. The ones on the wall seem to only capture the highlights though.

"You okay?" Alex asks.

I hadn't realized I had stopped at the prom picture. "Who is this I'm with?" I don't remember seeing him in any of the albums.

Alex frowns, "That's Blake. He was your boyfriend."

*Was?*

"I had a boyfriend?" Funny, they never mentioned that before. I guess they didn't want to upset me. Did he break up with me after the accident? What kind of guy breaks up with his girlfriend when she's in a coma? I zero in on the picture some more. He's a nice looking guy, looks athletic. Dark hair, dark eyes. Taller than me, though everyone is really. We look happy.

"That was from his senior prom. He was a year ahead of us. He broke up with you before he went off to college." The frown on Alex's face looks misplaced on his usually chipper appearance. In the month that I've known him, I'm not sure I've seen any negative expressions on his face, other than sadness in our initial visits when even *he* couldn't break through the force field guarding my brain.

"Oh. I didn't go to my senior prom?"

"Nah, you weren't dating anyone and had already been to three proms, so you said screw it, and hung out with the band instead. We had a gig that night for the non-prom folks. It was awesome."

"I went to three proms?" Wasn't I just the social butterfly?

Alex nods, seeming uncomfortable that I'm still asking about this. "You went to your junior prom, and Blake's junior and senior proms."

"We were together that long?" I had a relationship spanning at least a year and they never mentioned it? How could they have left out such a big chunk of my life in high school? They shared so much other stuff.

"You guys dated your sophomore and junior years." He seemed to consider his next statement before speaking it, which is also very not Alex. "You were pretty messed up when he left you. That's why we didn't tell you about it. Didn't want to open up old wounds."

"How'd you know I was wondering about that?"

He taps his head and grins, "twintuition."

I smile and roll my eyes. "You're such a goof." I take one last look at the picture, and proceed up the stairs behind him.

"That's yours, second one on the right. It's smaller than the rest, but it's got the biggest closet. Apparently, that was essential." Now it's his turn to roll his eyes, and I smile in return. From what I've been told, I'm beginning to realize I was a tad bit spoiled, both by my brothers and my parents.

I step past him into the room. The carpet is shaggy and a deep purple in color, and the walls are painted a much lighter shade of the same color. There's a full-sized bed with a bookcase, headboard, a matching nightstand, wide dresser with a round mirror, and a narrow dresser with a hutch. All have a shiny black finish. Band posters are hanging on the walls, along with a corkboard with miscellaneous things attached, including more photos. I make a beeline for it. Pictures are worth a thousand words and all that. Looks like there are some mementos tacked up there, too.

There are photos here of me, Alex, and Trevor. There are also pictures of my parents, a few of Alex and Trevor with a couple good-looking guys I know must be their bandmates, and some of me and a girl I vaguely recall my brothers pointing out in my yearbook. A few ticket stubs are scattered, some from sporting events but most from concerts. I startle when I feel Alex's presence behind me.

"Sorry," he says.

"It's okay," I tell him. "Who is that?" I point to the girl.

"That's Lucy; she was your best friend. I think I pointed her out in our yearbook." There's that "was" again. He says it so nonchalantly that I wonder whether or not there's a story there.

"Was?"

"Well, she kind of bailed on you. Not sure if you could call her a best friend anymore." He shrugged. Again, so nonchalant. I wonder, do I have anyone left? Besides Alex and Trevor? My boyfriend dumped me, my parents died, and my best friend bailed.

"Did she bail before or after the accident?" I wonder out loud.

"Not really sure. You hadn't been spending much time with her before, at least that I noticed. You spent most of your time with us. Lucy came to the hospital after the accident and she visited with us a few times while you were in ICU. But then the doctors said 'coma' and a couple weeks went by...she just stopped coming. She never visited you when you were at the long-term care facility."

"Oh." How sad. Here I am, fresh out of a coma, no memories and apparently no friends. Thank God I have my brothers.

"She went away to college, California, I think," he continues. "So that could be why she disappeared. And then we were on our tour so I don't know if she ever came back to North Carolina. Haven't seen her around. That's the band," he points to the picture of him and Trevor with the two guys.

"Chase and Joey," I say, remembering their names from Alex and Trevor's ridiculous and hilarious stories. They must be some group when they are all together.

"Yep," Alex smiles. "That one's Joey," he points to the shortest of the four, the one with the beard. "And that's Chase," he points at the blue-eyed blond, between Trevor and Alex in height. Both are attractive, but Chase... Chase is gorgeous. Those eyes. I half expect to see the sun shining in them; they are the perfect color of sky.

"Will I meet them?" I hope I will meet *him*.

"Heck, yeah," Alex grins and nods.

"In due time," Trevor says from the doorway. I spin quickly to look at him, I didn't realize he was standing there. He had brought up the last of my bags from the car and they were sitting by his feet in the doorway. "We don't want to overwhelm you, and, well, they can be overwhelming."

"*Joey* can be overwhelming," Alex corrects. "Chase doesn't do anything."

"He doesn't do anything?" I question, beginning to feel like a parrot.

"Chase is the strong, silent type," Trevor says. "Joey has the energy of a toddler. Bet you can guess who was friends with who first?" I laugh, the descriptions of Joey and Chase are just as I've described Alex and Trevor in my head.

"You'll probably see Chase around here sooner rather than later, though," Trevor informs me. "He lives in the apartment over the garage."

I nod; I won't exactly mind seeing him around. At least, I don't think I would mind. Can't tell them that though.

"They know to give you some time," Alex adds. "But I also know they're just dying to see you, so don't be surprised if we're ambushed. They've missed you, too. Joey's wife, Evie, is really looking forward to having another chick around."

"Was I friends with Evie?" I ask. I don't recall the name being connected with any pictures in the albums they had shared. But they may have mentioned it once or twice. I am experiencing information overload no matter how simply they convey information to me. But at least I'm not overwhelmed or anxious. Just processing. Always processing.

"No, you've never met her. She and Joey met at one of the stops on the tour and have been inseparable ever since," Trevor answers.

"Crazy ass shit," Alex shakes his head in mock disgust. "That girl's a firecracker though, a lot like you actually."

"Yeah, you two will probably get along great," Trevor agrees. "Which will be good for both of you since neither of you really know anyone around here." He winces, "Sorry. That was a little callous."

I shake my head. "No, it wasn't; it's the truth. I don't really know anyone, not yet anyway. It'll be nice to make a new girlfriend since apparently my old one has disappeared. Lucy," I add when he tilts his head in question. He nods in response, looking sad for me.

Alex walks over to the bedroom door and stops beside Trevor. "Enough of this heavy shit. I'm going to put my shorts on and get in the pool."

"We have a pool?" I ask, my eyes wide. I'm not really sure why this excites me so much.

"Yep, it used to be your favorite place." Well, maybe that explains it.

I look at Trevor, worrying my lower lip between my teeth. "I don't know if I can swim."

Alex lets out a great big laugh and clutches his stomach. "You were an award-winning swimmer! Of course you can swim."

"But what if I don't remember how?" I cringe as I hear my own whine. But I'm seriously nervous about getting in the pool. I want to, so badly, but is swimming just like riding a bike? You never forget? Or will I get in the water and sink like a lead weight?

"Only one way to find out," Trevor smiles. "Check your dresser drawers, one is bound to be full of swimsuits."

Trevor spins around and closes my bedroom door behind him. I turn and look around the room slowly, taking everything in a second time. I like the room, the colors and the furniture. I can see myself being comfortable here. It's all still a bit overwhelming, but at least I have a sense of comfort. That's got to be important. Dr. Moody did tell me to trust my gut.

I walk over to the narrow dresser and open up the top drawer. Bingo, full of swimsuits. He wasn't kidding, I must have been a fish in my previous life. I dig through and pull out the most modest one I can find, a black tankini suit. The color is going to completely drown out my pale skin, but whatever. It's not like I need to dress to impress my brothers.

Little did I know...

# Chapter Three

Less than fifteen minutes later, I'm floating on an inner tube in the large, kidney shaped pool, centrally placed in an enormous backyard, while Alex shoots a small basketball into a poolside net. Trevor stands at the impressively large, stone-surrounded grill, another small sign that men inhabit this place, prepping it in some guy way so he can make us some steaks for dinner.

"So what's your band's name again?" I absently ask Alex. I know they have mentioned the name in passing, but I can't remember what it is.

"JACT," Alex says as he slam dunks the basketball.

"Jacked? As in 'hijack' or 'carjack'?" I lift an eyebrow at him.

He smiles, "Think we're criminals, sis? Why can't it mean that we're all 'jacked up'?"

I roll my eyes. "Whatever. Will you just tell me why you named your band that?"

"Well, for one thing, it's not 'jacked,' J-A-C-K-E-D; it's JACT," he says sounding out the T. "J-A-C-T."

I sigh, sometimes getting information out of Alex is like pulling teeth. "That doesn't really explain anything."

"It's our initials," Trevor calls out, putting an end to my misery.

I think about it. J-Joey, A-Alex, C-Chase, T-Trevor. Makes sense. "That's actually kind of clever," I finally say, nodding.

Trevor laughs, "*You* would think so."

"What's that mean?" I ask.

"You came up with it," Alex says from behind me.

*Huh.* Well, how do you like that? "And you guys just accepted it?"

Trevor closes the lid on the grill so it can warm up and walks over to sit on one of the chaise lounges lined up alongside the pool. I paddle around in my tube so I can give him my full attention. He doesn't talk much, so when he does, I listen.

"Back when we fooled around in the garage," he begins, "we didn't have a name. We were just messing around. We didn't expect anything to come of it. Then one of dad's friends was over for dinner and heard us jamming out. He owned a restaurant out by the airport and featured live acts once a week. He liked what he heard and offered us a spot."

"But we didn't have a name," Alex inserts.

Trevor nods in agreement, "One of the first things he asked was what we called ourselves. We felt like total morons for not having a name for our band." He chuckles at the memory.

"So how did I end up naming the band?" I wonder out loud. From what I understood from their stories, I hung around with them a lot, more so in the year before the accident. So I guess it isn't too surprising that I had had a hand in naming their band, but I still want to hear the story.

"You should have heard some of the things those bozos were throwing out there," Trevor laughs. "The Orgasm Donors, which was classic since you were both a couple of sixteen year old virgins." I blush at the sexual reference, but laugh along with him, assuming he's talking about Alex and Joey.

"What about your suggestion, huh?" Alex teases right back. "Four Dudes." I laugh at that, too. Straight and to the point, very Trevor.

"An obvious choice," Trevor defends, and I laugh some more.

"So anyway," Alex starts, "we spent a couple hours going back and forth, pretty much making a game out of who could come up with the worst name, when you finally piped up and said JACT."

"We liked it enough when we thought it was J-A-C-K-E-D, but when you spelled it out for us, we were completely sold." Trevor has a proud smile on his face.

"And just like that, a band was born," Alex says theatrically.

"I knew I thought it was clever for a reason," I say simply and smugly.

The guys both laugh and shake their heads.

"Hey, there's something I've been wondering," I start. Since we are talking about the band and all of us hanging out together, this is the perfect opportunity to address something I've been curious about.

"What's up?" Alex asks.

I look towards Trevor and ask, "Wasn't it ever weird for you to be hanging out with your younger brother and sister all the time?"

"Nah," Trevor says. "Don't get me wrong, y'all were pains in my ass when you were little," Trevor and I laugh, while Alex has a "who me?" expression of disbelief on his face. "But Mom and Dad always made sure the three of us spent time together. And honestly, I liked spending time with both of you as we got older. The age difference really didn't mean much because you liked the same stuff I did."

"Not many people can list their family as their best friends. We three were--are--lucky," Alex adds.

"It does seem pretty cool we were close like that," I smile at them both.

I recall some of the stories other residents of the facility shared during group, and many of them had very broken relationships with their families, or broken families in general. It makes me appreciate what I have. Even though I don't remember my family's dynamic, it must have been pretty special for my brothers to have stuck by me, especially without my parents to guide them and keep us all together.

After a little more small talk, Trevor goes back to the grill, and I continue floating, leaning my head back and closing my eyes to block out the sun's harsh rays. My sunglasses are doing absolutely nothing to shade my eyes. August in Charlotte was proving to be brutal. I probably should put more sunscreen on my too white skin, but Trevor and Alex seem tan enough so hopefully my skin will bronze like theirs rather than burn.

I zone out for a little while, making mental lists of things I should do. I will need to go clothes shopping as I have apparently lost some weight. The size eight clothes my brothers had brought to the facility for me hang off my frail frame. The great coma diet. I don't have any money, at least I don't think I do, but something tells me that isn't going to be a problem.

Suddenly Alex shouts, jerking me out of my own head. "Yo, Baker!"

I follow Alex's gaze and see an Adonis. Short blond hair–but still long enough that I want to run my hands through it, eyes as blue as the sky, a slight smirk, tall, tan and muscled body. Yummy. This is Chase. I'd recognize those eyes anywhere. I hope he can't tell I'm staring at him, but as his smirk widens, I know he can. *Shit.* I'm sure he can also see the blush on my pale skin, but I try to convince myself that he thinks it's just heat from the sun.

I lay my head back against the tube again and pretend to be indifferent. Alex continues to shoot hoops beside me. After a few moments, which seem like hours, I chance another look at Chase. He's still in conversation with Trevor, but every few seconds his eyes sneak a peek at me. My face heats up again instantly.

I can't believe I'm having this reaction to him. He's the first guy I'm not related to that I've come into contact with since leaving the facility, and I'm ready to jump him. And he's twenty feet away! I feel like a little school girl with a crush. I wonder if Blake ever made me tingle on the inside and blush on the outside.

I float over to Alex as gracefully as I can. "He keeps looking at me," I whisper. I'm not sure why I share this information with my twin, but I do. I can only hope he can't detect the heat in my cheeks, because that would be embarrassing! Or if he does, I hope he doesn't figure out the reason.

"Al, the last time he saw you, you were unconscious. For a long time," he states in an obvious tone. He might as well have added 'duh' to the end of that statement.

"So?" I weakly argue. "Surely he has seen a girl before."

Alex laughs, "Yeah, I'm sure he has." I don't know why his comment bothers me, but it does. Just how many girls does Chase see? He is a rock star, after all. And why is it any of my business?

Alex quits messing around with his ball and turns to me, hanging over the side of my tube. "You were a fixture in all our lives, Al. Then one day you weren't. We were even with you that night, before you drove off with Mom and Dad. It was hard. On all of us. You were a part of the band, in a way, but it was more than that. We were all a family." He looks down for a moment, and when he looks back up it looks like he has tears in his eyes. It makes my heart hurt. "When Mom and Dad died, it gutted Joey and Chase, too. They were the only positive adult influence those two had. And with you being in limbo," Alex continues, "it was rough. They were both dealt a shit hand when it comes to family. Our family was all they had. And it broke with you guys gone. We all broke."

It makes me so sad to hear how much they had all suffered, and part of it was because of me. Even though it wasn't my fault, and there's nothing I ever could have done to change it, apart from wake up, I still felt responsible. Like if my body was stronger, I wouldn't have been in a stupid coma and I wouldn't be without my memory now. I want to hug Alex, Trevor, Chase and Joey. Tell them everything will be okay, but what do I know? I didn't even know my name a few weeks ago.

Before I can say anything deep or emotional, Alex does what Alex does. He grins deviously and flips my tube. "Damn it, Alex!" I shriek once I surface, spitting water out of my mouth and slapping my hands against the surface of the water. "I could have drowned!"

Alex is a couple feet away from me, laughing so hard he's struggling to tread water. "You're an All-State swim champ, you won't drown."

"Swimmers can drown!" I retaliate.

"Do you think I'd let you drown? You have no argument."

I growl and lunge at him, trying to dunk him under the water which only makes him laugh harder. I'm no match to his burly physique, and I have to admit, my weak attempts are pretty funny. Eventually, I'm laughing, too, as I hang on his back with my arms around his neck.

"I can so choke you right now," I warn him teasingly, which brings on more hysterics from both of us.

Having forgotten we've an audience, I look over to the grill where Trevor and Chase are standing, watching us. Both of them are smiling and shaking their heads at our antics. "Some things never change," I think I hear Chase say.

"You guys having a party and didn't invite me?" a new voice calls out just before a giant splash erupts beside me, splashing water in my eyes and up my nose. Apparently Alex was smart enough to turn his head or hold his breath, because he's completely unaffected as I cough and spit water out over his shoulder.

"Y'all know how he is. Damn dog with a bone, I tell you. Sorry, sweetie," a petite blonde with a pixie cut smiles at me as she calls out from the back door. She's absolutely adorable with a major southern twang going on, but all I can think of is how happy I am there's another fun-size person like me amongst all these giants.

"Al, that's Evie, and this doofus," Alex explains as said doofus surfaces beside me, "is Joey." The final band member and his wife. I recognize him now that I see him, but I haven't seen any pictures of her yet.

"Damn! Look at you girl!" His smile brightens his entire bearded face, brown eyes sparkling, and I can't help but smile back, it's infectious. "Come here," he says as he grabs hold of my arms and somehow pulls me over Alex's shoulder and into his chest for a big bear hug. I tense for a moment, but relax almost immediately. I feel safe, comforted, in Joey's arms. Kind of like how I feel with Alex and Trevor. Wonder how I'd feel in Chase's arms...

"Joey!" Evie shrieks, thankfully breaking my thought process before it went somewhere it probably shouldn't go. "I'm sorry y'all. I tried to keep him away, but I just couldn't. He was just too excited to see for himself that Ally was home." With her hands on her hips, she's shaking her head, and doing a very good impersonation of a disappointed parent.

"It's all good, Evie," Trevor assures her. "Kind of figured we couldn't keep him away too long. But maybe he could give her some breathing room!" He said the last bit a little louder; I suppose in an attempt to get Joey to pay attention.

Joey pulls back with his hands on my shoulders, looks into my eyes, and shakes his head. "Damn, it's good to see you."

"It's good to see you, too?" I say, though it comes out as a question. He laughs like that's the funniest thing he's ever heard and pulls me in again.

"Dude, back off," Alex scolds with a frown. "I haven't even hugged her yet and she's *my* sister." I swear if his feet could touch the bottom of the pool, he'd probably stomp them.

"Quit being a baby," Joey responds. He lets me go, but keeps looking at me. After what Alex said when I caught Chase looking at me, I'm not weirded out by Joey's stare. I understand that he's just happy to see me amongst the living.

"Joey, give the girl some space," Evie tells him.

Joey backs up a little, and I see that he's fully clothed. It makes me laugh. "You have all your clothes on!"

"Not the first time, probably won't be the last," Chase says, I look at him quickly and find he's looking right at me. I feel myself get warm again.

"Probably not," Joey admits. "Al," he pulls me into his side, earning a glare from Alex. "I want you to meet my wife. Evie, this is Al."

"It's so nice to meet you, finally," she says to me with a friendly smile. "Sorry about this one. He just couldn't wait another minute."

"It's okay. The guys have been telling me all about you two; I'm glad I got to meet you."

I *am* glad I got to meet another girl. It seems the old Ally surrounded herself with testosterone, and that was all well and good, but I think I need some she-time, too.

"I wish we could stay longer," Evie says regretfully, "but I've got to take this moron back home to change so we can make it to our appointment on time. Come on, ya big goof."

"You finding out what you're having today?" Trevor asks.

"No, not until closer to twenty weeks, this is just a standard checkup," Evie answers.

I drop my gaze to her stomach. Sure enough there's a tiny bump I'd completely missed before. "Congratulations," I tell her.

"Thanks, sweetie. We'll stop by again soon," she smiles, then turns back on her disappointed parent face. "Joseph! Out! Now!" We all laugh. I like this girl. The guys were right; she's a firecracker.

Joey swims back over to me from where he was talking with Alex and gives me another hug, this one quick. "So good to see you, lil' sis." He winks and lifts himself over the side of the pool, his clothes dripping with water.

"There are some extra towels over there," Alex says, pointing over to the chair by the door. "And you can run up to my room if you want, grab a change of clothes."

"Thanks, man. See y'all later!" Joey calls as Evie waves. Then they disappear back into the house.

I pop back up on my float, and as I adjust myself into a comfortable position, I catch Chase staring at me out of the corner of my eye. I boldly turn to face him and quietly gasp at what can only be described as desire in his eyes. Oh, boy. I am in so much trouble.

***

Shortly after Joey and Evie leave, Trevor announces that dinner is ready and that Chase is joining us, which is both a blessing and a curse. I want to spend more time with this glorious creature, but at the same time, I would rather not look like a drowned rat. I didn't have time to shower and change after the pool because Trevor finished grilling while I was still in the pool, and he insisted I not wait and have my steak get cold. I can't exactly argue my side with my brother.

I'm formally reintroduced to Chase as we sit down for dinner, and I feel a spark when he takes my hand in his. The strange, yet very brief, look he has on his face makes me hope he felt it, too, but I can't be sure. I keep stealing glances at him throughout dinner, and catch him looking back once or twice. I can't say that it doesn't thrill me to see that I may have a similar impact on him as he does on me.

I catch Alex looking between Chase and me near the end of the meal, and I worry I've been caught gawking at Chase. *Shit. What am I doing?* Chase is their friend. Their brother. Does that mean he's like my brother? Gross, I don't want to think about that. Chase is *not* like my brother! But how can I so blatantly disrespect my brothers like that, by crushing on the first single friend they introduce me to? I can't be one of *those* sisters.

I vow in that moment that I *will* get over my little infatuation with Chase Baker. Too much can go wrong, and too much is at stake.

# Chapter Four

It's the end of August and I've been home for almost a month. I do my best to avoid Chase, though it's hard since he lives in the apartment above the garage. Apparently it was an empty space, but after my parents died, the boys finished it, and Chase moved in. I see him around the house and property often, but I never make eye contact or speak to him, and I avoid any situation that can potentially leave us alone together. This results in a lot of time spent with Alex, Joey, and Evie, since Chase and Trevor are close and hang out together a lot. But apparently this is what it was like before the accident, minus Evie, so my behavior doesn't come off as avoidance. Plus, they're good company, and I have a great time with them, so I can't complain.

I feel comfortable around the house but have found my home in the kitchen. I stumbled upon it that first night I was home and immediately fell in love with the black granite countertops and stainless steel appliances. I stood, running my hands over the cool surfaces, just taking it all in until Alex wandered in and called me a freak.

I've discovered I love to cook and to bake. While I was bored one day, I browsed cookbooks and recipe cards and selected several that sounded delicious and looked simple enough for me to test out since I have no memory of having ever made a grilled cheese, let alone a recipe from scratch. I made a list of ingredients, knowing I'd have been lucky to find eggs and milk in the bachelors' refrigerator, and asked Trevor to take me shopping. He happily obliged and this has become a weekly ritual for us, our sibling bonding time. It's nice to spend that time with him. Since I'm spending most of my time with the others, I don't want him to feel like I'm avoiding him. I'm just avoiding his friend.

I seem to have found my purpose in cooking the guys dinner and dessert every night. Chase, Joey, and Evie join us occasionally, but it's Wednesday nights--when it's just me, Trevor, and Alex—that I'm happiest. My brothers insisted we have one night a week that was just family. Although I still can't remember anything, these dinners allow me to imagine what life was like before, when our mom and dad were here. On family nights, the seats at each head of the table remain vacant.

*** 

I'm in the kitchen mixing together batter for a gooey butter cake, when a figure in my peripheral vision startles me. I drop the mixing spoon and spin around quickly to see who it is.

"Trev, you nearly scared me to death!" I hold my hand up over my heart and feel it thumping in my chest.

"Sorry, kid," he says, but makes no motion to move. He has the strangest expression on his face. Something is off.

"Is there something wrong?"

"That song you were just humming, what is it?" He tilts his head to the side, as if considering what my response might be.

I didn't even realize I had been humming a song. "I don't know; I don't remember." I shake my head. "I was humming?"

"Yeah," he says quietly, his eyes piercing into mine, searching for something.

"What's up?" Alex asks as he walks in from the patio, his board shorts still dripping from the pool. His brows furrow as he senses the tension. The tension I don't understand myself.

"Ally was just humming 'Our Moon'," Trevor tells him.

Alex's eyes widen. "What? Are you sure?"

"Yeah," Trevor says. They continue to speak, now in hushed tones, back and forth, sneaking glances at me every few seconds. I can't make out what they're saying, and it's starting to freak me out.

"Um, will someone please tell me what's going on?" I beg, crossing my arms across my chest in a defensive gesture.

If there's anything worse than losing my memory, it's feeling left out almost all the time. I know it's not intentional, but sometimes the guys will get to talking and not realize that I don't recall any of the inside jokes that I may have been privy to a year and a half ago. I already feel bad enough that they have to give me an intro to practically every conversation they have since I don't know the back stories, even though they insist it's no big deal.

But this, this whispering about me, I don't like this feeling at all. It's making me feel anxious.

Trevor and Alex quit their quiet conversation and look over at me. "Did you hear that recently?" Trevor presses.

"I really didn't realize I was humming. I don't even remember the song," I say, beginning to feel like I've done something wrong. "Maybe I heard it on the radio or something."

"That's one of our songs," Alex says. "But we never recorded it."

"So maybe it was a subconscious memory?" I offer, perking up a little. Dr. Moody, who I still see weekly, said little things could start to make appearances here and there. Maybe this was one of them?

"It was written while you were in the coma," Trevor supplies.

I visibly deflate. "I guess I must have heard it since then," I shrug as I start drawing into myself. I'm feeling very uncomfortable now. Very out of place.

"We don't play that song," Alex states.

Trevor and Alex are standing side by side now in the doorway, searching my face for answers. I feel myself crumbling under their scrutiny. I start to feel the slow vibrations of an incoming anxiety attack. I've had a few since coming home, mostly when I feel the pressure of trying to remember. Dr. Moody tells me it will get better with time and that I have to stop pushing myself and punishing myself.

I rub my hands up and down my arms, trying to soothe myself as I start to lose my breath. "I'm s-sorry," I pant out. I know it will take only seconds before I feel like I'm suffocating. I heave a heavy breath in before dropping to my knees on the kitchen floor and folding in on myself next to my abandoned spoon and the cake batter splashed around it on the tile floor.

"What the hell happened?"

"I don't know, she was fine one minute; we were talking, and then she started having an attack."

I feel a warm hand running up and down my back and tingles in my spine. That's a new symptom. "Take deep breaths, Ally. Deep breaths." I try to listen. I can't make out who is speaking to me. The voices sound like they're under water.

"In and out, Ally. Breath in, breath out. Come on." I focus on that voice. Calm, soothing. I measure my breaths against the voice, the movements of the hand on my back.

"What upset her?"

"She was humming."

"That's good, Ally, in and out," the soothing voice says to me. Then to someone else it asks, "And that got her upset?"

"No, she was humming 'Our Moon'."

The hand on my back freezes for a moment, then continues. "So?"

"How does she know that song?"

"So what, you interrogated her?" The soothing voice is angry now. "Keep breathing, baby girl," he quietly whispers to me. The underwater tone is disappearing.

"Shit, I didn't mean to."

"What the hell, man?"

"I'm sorry, Al." That's Trevor.

"Me too, little sis." And Alex.

I don't answer. My breathing is under control now, and I feel embarrassed. Because now I recognize the third voice, the soothing one. Chase. I just broke down in front of Chase. I've been avoiding him for weeks, and this is how we are reunited? Annoyed, I nudge what I assume is his hand off of my back and twist up from the floor, facing away from them. I'm sure I have tears and possibly snot on my face, as is often a result of my anxiety attacks. I don't want *him* to see me like this.

"I'm fine," I mumble and run off to my room before anyone can reach me. Falling face first into my bed, I cry. I cry because I'm embarrassed. I cry because I can't remember, and I want to. So, so desperately. I cry for my brothers because they have to put up with me. And most of all, I cry because, while I'm so lucky and happy to be alive, I'm so incredibly frustrated.

After what feels like hours, but is probably only minutes, there's a knock on my open door. "Can we come in?" Trevor asks.

I roll onto my back, and through tear-soaked eyes, I look at my brothers nod. They look about as bad as I feel, and their faces drop even more now that they've seen the tears on my face. I know I look horrible, thanks to the ugly cry I just had.

They come into my room, and Alex flops down on his back beside me, while Trevor sits down on my left.

"Ally, I'm so sorry for putting you on the spot like that," Trevor says. Before I can interrupt and tell him it's okay, he says, "It is *not* okay that I did that."

"I'm sorry, too, Al." Alex adds. "There's no excuse for our behavior, it was just an odd song choice is all. Kind of freaked us out."

"Yeah, we were puzzled more than anything. I was just trying to ask about it without getting you excited about a possible memory or something. I didn't mean to make it seem like we were accusing you of something." Trevor reaches down, takes my hand and squeezes.

"Chase explained everything, and it makes sense now," Alex says. The sorrow in his voice matches his face. I reach my right hand over and take his hand in mine.

Wait a minute. Rewind. Chase explained everything? Huh? "What do you mean? About Chase?" I ask.

"He said he plays it sometimes. Said you probably heard it through the windows when you were out back or something. I'm sorry I freaked out and confronted you like that," Trevor says. I can tell he's really beating himself up over this. He's the level-headed one. He's always so thoughtful, he never reacts, and he's so meticulous. The fact that he had reacted without thinking, possibly for the first time in his adult life, is apparently causing him devastation.

"It's okay, I guess I can see how it would have seemed weird that I was humming that song." I squeeze his hand back in an effort to reassure him. "But please, tell me about this song. What is it about this song that caused you to freak out?"

"It's not really the song. I mean it is, but it isn't."

"Trev, that doesn't really clear things up," I snicker.

He sighs. "Chase wrote the song. He wrote it while you were in the coma. We all worked on it together really, but we've never played it in public and we never recorded it. It was just kind of odd that the one song of ours you hum happens to be the one no one has ever heard."

"Yeah, I mean 'Fall Down' we'd understand, It's has the most airtime on the radio. But 'Our Moon' has zero airtime. Zero play time at all, really," Alex explains.

"Should have known you might have heard it from Chase," Trevor shakes his head. "I really didn't mean to interrogate you like that, I just didn't really know how to ask about it without kind of freaking out. I guess."

"What's it about?" I wonder out loud.

"Chase hasn't ever said specifically, but it's not hard to figure out," Trevor says.

"The one that got away," Alex adds.

"A girl?" I ask. I'm not really sure I want to know the answer to that question. Kind of ruins the fantasy for me if there's a girl in Chase's life or his heart.

"Seems that way," Trevor responds. "Chase is very private, so we don't press him about it. His mom pretty much screwed him up as far as relationships go, too, so it's a rough topic in general. Pair that with him actually taking a chance and it backfiring, no good."

"No bueno," Alex says.

What did his mom do? I remember Alex saying that Chase and Joey had bad home lives, but he didn't share anything specific. I guess it's really not my business, but I just want to know everything I can about Chase. Something about him has been pulling me in since I first saw his picture.

"So," I begin, trying to lighten the mood, "did you think I have ESP or something? A sixth sense? I don't think I was floating around outside my body while I was in a coma."

"I don't know what I thought," Trevor says solemnly.

"Look, it's okay. Really. I'm going to have anxiety attacks over stupid shit. Don't beat yourself up over it."

"We just didn't mean to upset you and make you cry," Alex says.

I shake my head, "I'm just embarrassed. It was embarrassing. I can't engage in a simple confrontation without freaking out. It's humiliating. Why can't I just have simple reactions and interactions?"

"You've been through a lot, kid. You're entitled to some high quality freak outs."

"Thanks," I laugh. "I'm glad you condone my behavior."

Trevor lies back on the bed, and the three of us quietly stare at the ceiling fan for a while. I can't help but feel lucky and content, despite my earlier episode, being here with my brothers beside me.

Then Alex goes and breaks the silence. "Knock knock."

"Who's there?" Trevor answers.

"Dwayne."

"Dwayne who?" I chuckle. I have no clue where this was going, and knowing Alex, it can go anywhere.

"Dwayne the tub, I'm drowning!"

"Oh my gosh," I laugh. "You are such a dork!" Trevor just shakes his head, his usual response to Alex's antics. And just like that, the tension is broken.

# Chapter Five

*"Soon?" I ask.*

*"Soon," he promises.*

I wake from the dream in a peaceful state. How just two words spoken from deep within my subconscious can relax me so, I have no idea. I've been having random dreams since waking from the coma. Nothing that seems to mean anything, but many of them leave me feeling at peace, like this one.

There are a few different ones that seem to be on rotation. One was the one I've just woken up from, two words, the same word really, only spoken differently... *soon.* The second one is me in a dark hallway, there's nothing else but I recall a feeling of anticipation. Positive anticipation, if that makes sense. Like being eager and excited or something. The last one is a soothing melody. I often wonder if it's the song I was caught humming a couple weeks ago, but I don't dare ask.

I don't tell my brothers anything about my dreams because I don't know how they will react, and, well, I don't really want to know either. Things are going well between us, but that one day with the humming really shook things up for a little bit. It took about a week before Trevor stopped feeling awful about it, no matter how many times I assured him I was over it. I am over it, I just don't desire a repeat performance.

I save my dream talk for my appointments with Dr. Moody. I've been seeing her weekly since I was released, and I actually enjoy our sessions. Funnily enough, I feel like I can talk to Dr. Moody without her psychoanalyzing everything I say, and yet that's exactly what she's being paid to do.

"So you had another dream?" is her opening remark. We're sitting in the office of her private practice. It's where our sessions are held now that I'm out of the facility. I hadn't realized at the time that she just consulted with the facility, I thought she was there all the time. Her office there was a lot like this one. It was set up like a living room with a sofa, armchairs, and a desk set off to the side. There isn't any overhead lighting, just lamps set around the room providing a soft glow, similar to what you'd find at home. It's comfortable, and I know that's her goal.

"How did you know?" I ask, although I already know that she knows me better than I know me.

"You seem relaxed. Don't get me wrong, I'm not insinuating that you're always tense, but you're always more at peace after you've had a dream."

She hit the nail right on the head with that. "Yeah, I've actually had one every night for the past three nights."

"Lucky you," she smiles. "Which one?"

I've told her all about my dreams in hope that she can tell me what they mean. She isn't one of 'those dream shrinks,' and she told me just that when I first brought it up, but she is working with me to try to determine if the dreams are memories or just dreams. Sometimes dreams are just dreams. I have to remind myself of that almost daily to keep the anxiety, and hope, away.

"The one with the words," I tell her.

"*Soon*," she nods. "Did you feel any differently this time? Pick up on anything different? See anything, like the person you're speaking to or your environment?"

I shake my head. "Nothing at all."

"Since you've been meeting some more people, have you been able to recognize the other voice?"

I shake my head again. "We were whispering. I can just barely pick up that it's a male voice."

"Well, as you know, it may or may not be a memory. Sometimes memories manifest themselves in dreams. I know we've been over all this already, and I'm sorry we can't add anything new to that discussion. Do you want to talk about how you feel during and after the dream?"

"The same," I shrug. "Content. Peaceful. It's such a brief moment, though. I just wish I had a little more to work with."

"I know you do," she smiles. "We just have to be patient."

I'm running out of patience.

"So what else is going on?" Dr. Moody asks. "Still not driving?"

"I'm scared."

"It's understandable, you don't remember learning. Have you practiced at all?"

"Yeah, right. Trevor makes me nervous because he holds on to the side handle and the dashboard the entire time, stiff as a board, barking out commands. Then there's Alex, who can't take anything seriously and likes to crank the music up, scream randomly, and try to make me laugh, which doesn't help me calm down, at all."

Dr. Moody laughs. "Yes, I suppose neither of those are ideal situations to learn in. What about someone else? A friend? A driving school?"

"I thought about it, but I guess I don't feel I need to drive that badly, and I can just wait until the conditions are right." Or until I miraculously remember how to do it.

"Do you think your indifference, or reluctance, about relearning to drive has anything to do with the accident?" she asks.

I hadn't really thought about that. Perhaps it's a subconscious thing. Maybe somewhere deep inside of me remembers the accident and my lack of enthusiasm for the task stems from that. Maybe it's my body or mind's way of protecting itself. Though I wasn't driving that night, and I'm not afraid to be in a car. So who really knows?

"Do you think that's possible?"

"The mind is an amazing thing, and fear can be a very strong emotion. I like to think that anything is possible, and that seems to be very true when it comes to the mind."

Well, that was clear as mud.

"I just wish my mind would throw me a bone."

Dr. Moody smiles, "Indeed."

We move on to talk about how I've been spending my days and my future goals. When I talk about how I love being in the kitchen, she suggests the possibility of culinary school, and a future in that field. I worry about the expense, but she reminds me that my parents left behind a sizable estate, and I know my brothers aren't broke either. I still feel guilty taking money that I don't feel is mine, and I tell her that, so she suggests I get a job but still consider accepting financial support from my family.

I leave with homework: research opportunities for a future in cooking or baking, and discuss it with my brothers. She assures me they will be supportive of whatever I want to do, as long as it makes me happy. I'm pretty sure culinary school will make me happy.

***

Trevor drops me off at home after my appointment. He has to go meet the guys at the studio. They're working on recording their second album. Apparently they put it on hold when I woke up, and now that I'm home and doing well, they're moving along with it. Fortunately for them, the head of the label they signed with has been very supportive of their situation, i.e. me, and gave them some generous time off. But it's back to the grindstone for them now.

I welcome the peace and quiet at home and pull out my laptop to do some research. My new Dell is just one of the many endless gifts my brothers have bestowed upon me. I search for culinary schools in Charlotte and immediately come across The Art Institute. They have a degree program in Culinary Arts and a Certificate program in Baking and Pastry. I can do both, and I can do them close to home. I'm sold. That was easier than I thought it would be.

I gather information and take notes on the programs and the cost. I also map out the distance between home and the school, building my case to present to Trevor and Alex. I spend hours browsing the curriculum and course descriptions. There are techniques they teach that I've never even heard of, not that I'm a culinary genius or anything. But I'm getting excited. This is something I can do and something I will love. Something I can be passionate about.

When Trevor and Alex get home later that evening, they're not alone. Chase is with them. Do I want to have this conversation with Chase present? I don't know, but I'm practically vibrating with excitement so I can't possibly put it off until their marathon XBOX session is over.

I walk to the doorway of what I affectionately call 'the man room' and ask, "Can I talk to you guys for a minute?" Trevor and Alex look over at me with alarm. I suppose I've never taken such a serious tone with them before.

Chase speaks up, "I can go."

"No, it's okay," I tell him. And I think that's the first sentence I have actually spoken directly to Chase since I've been home. "It's nothing bad or personal." Trevor and Alex visibly relax. As does Chase. Odd.

"What's up, kid?" Trevor asks.

I am holding all my papers against my chest, and I can tell they're all curious as to what I've got in my hands. "As you know," I start out very formally, "I had my appointment with Dr. Moody today." They all nod and wait for me to continue. "She encouraged me to make future plans."

"What kind of plans?" Alex asks sharply. He's always had a love/hate relationship with Dr. Moody. He wasn't pleased that she kept them from me the first few days I was up out of the coma and was always worried she would talk me into staying at the facility or living in a group home or something. But he could still appreciate the benefits of my sessions with her. My progress has shown over the past few weeks.

"Chill out, bro. Let her talk."

I smile my thanks to Trevor and continue. "I want to go to culinary school," I blurt. I close my eyes tight so I that can't see their reaction. I don't know what I expect, but I'm nervous they'll laugh at me or tell me no.

I jump as I feel a hand on my arm. I open my eyes and look up at Alex. I didn't even hear him approach. And he's smiling. "That's awesome, little sis."

"It is?" I ask, not feeling any of my earlier confidence.

"Yeah, it is," he nods.

I look over to Trevor, "Do you think it's awesome?"

His usual serious expression fades into a smile, "I think it's a great idea. I think you'll do awesome in culinary school."

"You'd make a great chef, Ally," Chase says.

I look down and blush from Chase's praise. "Thanks, guys. Your support means so much to me." I show them the things I printed out and begin talking very animatedly. "I found a school here in Charlotte, The Art Institute. They have a Culinary Arts degree program *and* a Baking and Pastry certificate program. I downloaded all this information, and I really think I can do both." I continue to tell them all about the classes and how close the campus is. My excitement is palpable.

"That's so great, Al," Alex says, giving me a side hug. If I'm not mistaken, it looks like he has tears in his eyes. All the boys look a little somber.

"Are you guys okay? Is there something wrong? Do you not want me to go?"

"Everything is fine," Trevor says. "I promise. It's just that, well, it kind of feels like we're getting an old piece of you back is all." The other two nod their agreement.

"What do you mean?" I ask, looking each of them in the eye before moving to the next.

"Culinary school was your dream," Chase says. "Before."

My eyes dart back to his. Culinary school had been my dream? This is a positive thing, right? I chose the same future as I had before. It definitely has to be my subconscious. "Why didn't you guys tell me?"

"Dr. Moody didn't want us to overload you with too much information," Trevor says. "I guess we were all afraid if you knew about your plans from before, then you might try too hard to want those same things again and that could cause setbacks, or it might influence your decisions. You might have started doing things because you thought they were what you should have been doing. She thought it would be better if you steered your path on your own so that you would be making choices as the person you are now, not based off the person you were before."

"But I *am* the same person." And Dr. Moody is the one who suggested culinary school. Practice what you preach much?

"Yeah, and this kind of proves that," Alex smiles, then rolls his eyes. "But you know Dr.

Moody, she fully believes in the 'no pressure' methodology."

I nod, knowing he's right. "So you guys kind of knew this all along, huh? I mean when I began to spend all my time in the kitchen, you had to have had a clue."

Alex smirks. "Yep. We totally celebrated behind your back that first day when Trevor took you grocery shopping."

"Y'all are so sneaky," I laugh. "I can't believe you didn't invite me to the party."

"We'll invite you to the next one," Alex retorts.

"So you'll let me in on the secret if I do something else the old me would have done?"

"I guess so," he says.

"I'll help you out with the application for The Art Institute tomorrow," Trevor offers. "I bet I can dig up a copy of your old application in dad's office, or maybe the school still has it on file. You were accepted to the program already. Shouldn't be too difficult to get back in."

"Thanks," I smile, genuinely happy now that I have a goal in mind and knowing that I have their support.

"Mom and Dad would be real proud of you, too, Al." Trevor says quietly.

Tears come to my eyes as I nod in response.

"Wanna play with us?" Alex asks as he pulls out the controllers, thankfully breaking the somber moment.

"Nah," I say. "I'm just going to head up to bed and read for a little bit." I say my goodnights and go upstairs.

As I lay in my bed, I think about what just transpired. I don't know much about amnesia, aside from the few things Dr. Moody told me and what I read on the Internet, but I feel like this had to be a positive sign. I'm gravitating towards things I had previous interests in. Somewhere deep down, I'm still me.

# Chapter Six

I'm in the kitchen, taking a sheet of chocolate chip caramel cookies out of the oven, when Chase comes in the back door.

"Hey, Al," he says as he steps inside and wipes his feet on the doormat. It rained earlier in the day, and the patio is still wet.

"Oh, hey, Chase. The guys aren't home. Alex is with Joey, and Trevor just ran out to the store to get me an ingredient I forgot for dinner." I set the cookie sheet down on the hot pad and turn to face him as he pauses in his path to the man room and turns around.

"Okay, I guess I'll come back in a little while then." He gives me a shy smile and heads back to the door. For some reason, I don't want him to go. Since we spoke the handful of words to one another the night of my culinary school announcement, I haven't wanted to avoid him as much, but for some unknown reason, things still seem strained. Perhaps it's the fact that I ignored him for weeks after the pool/dinner incident.

"You can stay," I tell him quickly. "I don't mind. This is the last batch. I just need to put them on the cooling rack and then maybe we can go watch TV or something while you wait for the guys to get back?"

He looks at me like he's trying to figure something out, then nods his acceptance to my offer. "Okay, anything I can do to help?"

"I don't think so, thanks, though. Why don't you go find something to watch, and I'll be in there in a minute?" I pick up the small spatula I've been using to gently remove the cookies from the sheet.

He nods again, still looking at me strangely, and heads to the man room. I hear the TV turn on and finally exhale. I didn't even realize I was holding my breath. There's just something about him. I shake the feeling off, reminding myself that I can't even think about going there with my brother's best friend, my brothers' brother. But I can at least play nice with him.

I move the cookies from the sheet to the cooling rack. After plating a few and pouring a couple glasses of milk, I make my way to the man room with the tray full of goodies. Chase immediately gets up to help me, and I smile my thanks as I hand over the tray.

"These smell delicious," he says as he sets them down on the folding tray table I pulled out from the rack beside the entertainment center.

"Thanks, I came up with the recipe myself," I tell him. "Well, I picked apart a few different recipes to form this one recipe."

"So this is a Frankenstein cookie?" he asks as he lifts one to his mouth. That mouth... Full lips concealing perfectly white teeth. Sigh.

"Ha ha. If you're too afraid to try my concoction, you don't have to," I tease. Am I flirting with him? Stop it, Ally!

Chase grins, letting me know he was only teasing, and shoves the entire cookie in his mouth.

"Oh my gosh, that's so gross," I laugh.

He smiles as he chews. Then he closes his eyes and groans. And my heart. Just. Stops.

"This is so good, Ally," he moans through his chewing.

My mind is completely in the gutter now as I stare at him, completely unabashed. I'm sure if his eyes were open, instead of closed in cookie ecstasy, he would see the pure hunger I have for him, not the cookies, in my eyes as I sit here and imagine the various other situations where I would love to hear him say those words.

I try to shake it off but not before he opens his eyes and catches me staring at him. When his eyes widen, I know he sees what I was hoping he wouldn't. I catch a similar look in his eyes before I turn my head away and shove a cookie in my own mouth.

Not my best move, that's for sure, especially when I start choking on a crumb. I quickly swallow down the cookie in my mouth with a chug of milk and proceed to try and cough out the crumb.

Chase pats my back. "You okay?" he asks, concern etching his voice.

I nod as I take another sip of milk. "Wrong pipe," I rasp out.

Out of the corner of my eye, I swear I see a small grin on his face. I'm so embarrassed. If I thought it was embarrassing having Chase witness my anxiety attack, this is so much worse. First, he catches me looking like I want to eat him. Then, he watches me stuff a whole cookie into my mouth and proceed to choke on it. This is just great. Why can't I just be normal?

"There are some reruns of *Storage Wars* on TV, you used to love this show." I look over at him in shock. That's it? He isn't going to point out the obvious? He's just going to let it all slide and not say anything to further humiliate me? He looks from the television back to me and smiles his shy smile again. "Or we could watch *Overhaulin'*," he says, referring to the car show he and my oldest brother can't seem to get enough of.

I laugh, "*Storage Wars* it is." We sit in a surprisingly comfortable silence, eating cookies and watching Darrell and Jarrod battle it out over a locker that contains bedroom furniture of all things. But no matter how normal the setting, my mind won't stop racing. What I felt for Chase just then, I'd never felt that before, at least not in this life. It felt both good and bad at the same time. I really have to rein it in though, because nothing can happen there.

Chase must have noticed I was spending more time in my head than in the TV show because he touches his hand to my arm and asks, "You okay?"

"I'm fine," I answer, looking up from my lap to the TV. Nothing is wrong, aside from the electricity of his touch, that is.

"You know, if there's ever anything you need to talk about, you can talk to me. I know you don't know me that well, or you feel you don't, or whatever, but I'm here for you," he rambles. "I know I'm not one of your brothers, but if you ever feel you can't talk to them about something, maybe you can talk to me."

I consider what he's saying as I look into his endless blue eyes. For some reason, I want to be able to talk to him, to trust him. I nod my understanding, and he turns back to the TV. "There is something," I say quietly, and I have no idea why I'm even bringing this up after what my brothers told me about the song they'd caught me humming, the one that he confessed to playing.

He looks back to me immediately. "Anything. You can talk to me about anything," he says eagerly.

I look down to my lap again, "The song I was humming that day, the day I had the anxiety attack, and you came in." I look to him for recognition, and he looks a little tense, but he nods for me to go on. "Alex said you said you play it sometimes and that's probably how I'd heard it."

"Yeah," he agrees, but doesn't say anything else.

"Would you play it for me?" I ask softly, not wanting to overstep my bounds, but knowing full well I probably have. He doesn't say anything for a moment, and I quickly try to retract my question. "Never mind, forget I asked. It's silly."

"No, it's not silly. I'd love to. Play it for you, that is." I look at him and the expression on his face confuses me. He looks almost pained, but he's still so damn beautiful.

"Will you tell me about it?"

"What do you want to know?"

"Did you write it?" My brothers said he did, but I want to hear him tell me about it.

"Yeah. Well, the guys helped. But I did the lyrics and came up with most of the melody."

"Why haven't you recorded it?"

Now it's his turn to look down. "It's personal. It just didn't feel right at the time, not something I, we, wanted to share with the world. Maybe someday," he says as he looks back up into my eyes.

Gosh, they were right. It was personal. He must have written it about a woman, someone who he loved or who broke his heart, or both. And here I am, asking him to relive that for me. "You don't have to play it for me. It's personal, I get that. I've just been having these dreams," I realize what I've just said and stop talking immediately, closing my eyes tight. I can't believe I brought up the dreams!

"Dreams? What dreams?" he asks, lifting his right knee up on the couch and turning his body in to face me. I'm momentarily dazed by his proximity.

"It's nothing."

"It's something or you wouldn't have brought it up," he points out.

I sigh, knowing that he's right. I don't want to talk to my brothers about my dreams, but maybe I could talk to Chase. "There have been a few dreams since I got out of the coma. Recurring dreams I guess you could say. In one, there's a song. I just wonder if it's the same one."

"What are the other ones about?" he asks, that same strange look on his face.

"I don't want to talk about those," I say, quickly looking away.

He nods. "Okay. Well, I'll play the song for you. If it will help you, I'd be happy to do it."

I give him a small smile. "Thanks. I think it will give me peace of mind, you know? To be able to identify the song? And if it's not 'Our Moon,' then I'm back to the drawing board." Been hanging out there a lot lately.

He nods again, but doesn't say anything else. We return to watching TV in silence, leaving me to wonder when he'll play the song for me. I don't want to ask, as it already seems this won't be an easy thing for him to do and he's being kind enough to do it anyway.

Our silence is broken when Trevor returns from the store. I quickly thank Chase for keeping me company and hurry off to the kitchen to get started on dinner. When he's ready to play the song, he will come to me.

\*\*\*

As it turns out, I don't have to wait too long for Chase to come to me. That evening,

I'm lying in a chaise by the pool after dinner, just staring up at the moon and the stars. Alex is still out with Joey, and Trevor had a date, so I'm all alone at the house.

I startle when I hear footsteps approaching me, not sure of who it might be. I look over my shoulder and see Chase approaching with his guitar. "Hey," I say.

"Hey," he says back. He sits on the chaise beside mine, sets the guitar on his lap, and starts playing. No introduction, no nothing. He just sits down and begins.

The music, it's beautiful, and it's just what I remember from my dreams. But the lyrics, the lyrics are what I've been missing all this time. They complete the song and add a whole new range of emotions.

*Lying here with you,*

*It's better than I imagined it would be.*

*Waiting here with you,*

*How worthwhile I know it will be.*

*Under our moon,*

*Promises made.*

*Under our moon,*

*A love I wish had stayed.*

*Now you're gone,*

*But not that far away.*

*You'll come back,*

*It's all I ever pray.*

*Under our moon,*

*Promises made.*

*Under our moon,*

*A love I wish had stayed.*

*I'm left here missing you,*

*And no one understands.*

*The pain I feel every day,*

*It's all in someone else's hands.*

*Under our moon,*

*Promises made.*

*Under our moon,*

*A love I wish had stayed.*

*Baby, come back to me,*

*And happy we will be.*

*Baby, please,*

*Please just find your way,*

*Until then, forever yours I will stay.*

He doesn't hide the emotion in his eyes when he looks up at me as he finishes the song, the song that he sang like a plea. The man is clearly in pain, so I can tell there's truth behind the lyrics. Whoever this woman is, I'm not so sure she deserves him, if she left him like the song clearly insinuates. I want to know everything about this song, but I don't have the heart to ask him to open wounds that are obviously still so fresh.

He looks at me for another moment before nodding once, getting up, and walking off. I sit there, stunned at his abrupt departure, watching his retreating form, before lying back on the chaise and looking up at the night sky again.

For some reason, the moon looks different than it did a few moments ago.

# Chapter Seven

Trevor worked some magic with The Art Institute, and I'm able to begin classes in the fall term, which is beginning in just a few weeks. Evie and I have a shopping trip planned this weekend so I can get a 'back to school' wardrobe. I'm looking forward to having some girl time with her. The guys were right; Evie and I get along great. But with her job--she's a photographer--we don't get to hang out that often. That's okay with me because when we do get together it's more of a treat.

I'm sitting on the comfy couch in the living room reading ahead in one of my text books when the doorbell rings. This has sort of become my room, like the boys have their man room. I save my place in the book and make my way through the foyer to the front door. Peeking through the peephole, I see it's Chase. Well, that's odd. He usually comes right in.

"What's up?" I ask as I open the door. He seems nervous, shuffling from one foot to the other.

"I, uh, I was just wondering what you were up to." He's looking down, not making eye contact. He has always come off as a little shy to me, but he's usually a bit more confident than this.

I tilt my head to the side, trying to figure him out. "I'm just reading," I tell him. "Want to come in?"

"Yeah," he says. I pull the door open wider, and he steps past me into the house. "What are you reading?"

"Just a little bit of my textbook for class." I close the front door and walk back to the living room. I can hear his quiet footsteps behind me. I get a secret thrill knowing he's following me, and that he came over here for me in the first place. I do a quick check of my attire as I walk. Denim cut-offs, pink tank top, bra, all clean. Good. I take a seat on the couch and gesture for him to sit beside me.

"I'm not interrupting you, am I?" he asks as he sits down awkwardly.

"No, I could probably use a break anyway. If I keep going, I'll be the only dork in my class who finished the book before classes even begin." I laugh a little at my own awkwardness.

"You're not a dork," he says quietly, still not making eye contact.

"Thanks," I smile shyly. It seems the awkwardness that was missing when Chase and I shared cookies has revealed itself once again. It has been mildly awkward between us ever since he sang that song to me a couple weeks ago. I've only seen him in passing, since the band is busy finishing the album, but when I have seen him, I've gotten a simple head nod, not even a "hi." He had said the song is personal. I know I shouldn't have pushed. Now he's probably embarrassed he bared his soul to me in that way.

"So... why did you ring the doorbell?" I might as well ask what I was thinking.

He looks up at me, then back down quickly. "I knew the guys weren't home, and I didn't want to startle you by just walking in. Plus, I wanted to ask if you wanted to hang out, and just coming right in would have been a bit presumptuous."

I'm a little high on the fact that he came over just to hang out with me; I'm definitely swooning on the inside. On the outside, I'm cool as a cucumber. I think.

"What do you want to do?"

He looks up at me and an adorable, boyish smile takes up his face. "You want to hang out?"

I laugh, "I let you in, didn't I? Why do you seem so surprised?"

He shakes his head. "I don't know. I guess things just seem a little weird between us lately."

"I know. I'm sorry I asked you to play the song." Now it's my turn to be shy and study my feet.

"What?" he asks. "No, don't be sorry."

I look up, and my gaze lands straight in his gorgeous eyes. "But that's when things got awkward. I mean we weren't exactly best buds before that or anything, but we hung out and watched TV together, and it seemed like we were going to be friends. Then I opened my stupid mouth and asked about the song. You said it was personal, and I should have just dropped it."

"Ally," Chase interrupted.

"Hmm?"

"It's okay. Really."

"It's *not* okay." I shake my head, getting upset. "We were going to be friends and then the song happened, and we haven't spoken in nearly two weeks."

He scoots closer to me on the couch, his left leg is touching my right leg. I swear I can feel that electric current buzzing through our bodies. "Hey," he says, bringing my stare from where our legs are meeting to his face. "Is that what you think? That we're not friends anymore?"

I shrug my shoulders, not really knowing what to say. I'm emotional and completely overreacting, but that's kind of par for the course as far as I'm concerned. I'm surprised I'm not having an anxiety attack, but something about Chase soothes me.

"Ally, I'll always be your friend. I'll never not want to be friends with you."

"Promise?" I ask on a sniff, doing a fine job at controlling my emotions, if I do say so myself.

"Oh, baby girl." In a very un-Chase-like move, he puts his arm around my shoulder and pulls me into his side. "Don't be sad. I promise I'm not going anywhere."

This is weird. Different. Unexpected. But I feel safe in his embrace, relaxed, so I pull my legs up on the couch beside me to make myself more comfortable. "Thanks."

"Anytime, baby girl."

"Why do you call me that?" I feel him tense, ever so slightly, but it's there.

"I don't know," he answers carefully.

"You called me 'baby girl' that day in the kitchen when I was having an attack." I feel him nod against my head. "I like it," I admit quietly.

"I like it, too," he says, then he kisses the top of my head, so softly I could have imagined it. But I am so aware of Chase's presence that I would probably feel it if he blew me a kiss from one hundred yards away. I can't stop the grin from forming on my face.

"So what do you want to do today?" he asks.

"This is nice," I say, still smiling and still curled up against him.

He pulls me in a little closer. "Yeah, it is." I'm glad I'm not the only one feeling it. Whatever *it* is.

"Sometimes I feel so alone," I confess to him after a few minutes of heavenly silence. "Some days, I'm surrounded by people, but I still feel like I'm all by myself. Like I'm not in on the jokes or the stories. It makes me really sad."

"I'm sorry you feel that way. I wish I could say 'you're not alone' and have you believe it, but I know it's probably going to be very hard for you to feel any differently as long as you don't have your memories."

I nod against his chest, a tear escaping my eye. It's like he knows just what to say.

"You sure you haven't had amnesia before?" I joke.

He laughs. "No, why?"

"Because that was a good answer. Or non-answer, rather."

"I just don't think it would do any good to coddle you or pretend that everything is going to be okay, when we all know it's a very real possibility that you may never get your memory back. We just need to help you through it and not try to fix everything."

I lean back and look at him questioningly. "You a psych major or something?"

He lets out a big laugh and pulls me back into his chest. "No. I might've read a couple books on amnesia since you've been diagnosed."

My breath catches. He did that? For me? "Wow, Chase. I don't know what to say."

"I just want to be here for you. As your friend, or whatever."

"Or whatever? What's that?" I ask, hoping the 'whatever' is something more, but knowing it's probably be too good to be true. I'm not sure if his silence is because he's considering my question, or ignoring me.

"That's yet to be defined," he finally answers. And while his answer is as vague as the initial statement was, it gives me peace anyway.

# Chapter Eight

On Saturday, Evie came to pick me up in her adorable little red Volkswagen Beetle for our shopping trip. The car suits her sassy personality to a T, especially the eyelashes over the headlights.

"Thank you so much for taking me shopping," I tell her. "Trevor or Alex would have, but shopping with them is just awkward. Either they get recognized, and we're swarmed, they complain that I'm taking too long, or they have something to say about every single thing I pick up."

Evie laughs, "I grew up with four older brothers. Trust me, I more than understand what it can be like."

I realize I don't know much about Evie, aside from her relationship with Joey and her ever present spark. "Are you from around here?" I ask her as she backs out of the driveway.

"Nope, Texas." I thought her accent was a bit different than the rest, more of a drawl than I've heard from the guys. "That's where Joey and I met, when they were playing a show in Dallas." "Playing" comes out like "playin.'" I could listen to her smooth drawl all day.

That's right, I remember the guys saying they met at a tour stop on the road, but I don't recall if they mentioned where. "Is your family still there? That's a long way from here."

"Yeah, they have a ranch. I was not cut out for that kind of life," she laughs, and I think to myself that I can't picture her on a ranch so I can see her getting out of there at her first opportunity. "I was always a city girl at heart, even though I sound totally country," she laughs, and I laugh with her.

"Do you miss them?" I wonder.

"I do," she nods. "I miss the people, not the place though. Joey and I've been back to visit a couple times since I left. So that helps."

"Do your parents approve of your relationship with him?" Not that it's any of my business, but nothing seems to offend Evie.

"They didn't in the beginning. My brothers were more of an issue, actually. But I sat them all down and told them how I felt. I've never been shy about my feelings, ever, so I just laid it all out. They knew I wasn't happy living on the ranch. That was a given. They all supported my need to see the world, but they weren't crazy about the fact that I'd found me a man to do it with."

I can imagine that Trevor and Alex would probably react the exact same way if I met a guy and wanted to basically run away with him. "So what changed?"

"They met Joey and saw the two of us together. My momma said it was like seeing two halves become a whole. She still wasn't crazy about me running away with him, but she could tell I was happy and she couldn't argue with that. Again, my daddy and my brothers were a tougher sell, but my momma told them to take a real look at me and how happy I was, and asked how they could try to get in the way of that? They couldn't, and they knew it. I was the baby, and they all did everything they could to make me happy. They were just sad that they maxed out their abilities, and I needed someone else to carry it on."

"That's kind of sweet," I say.

"It is. I love them all, and we talk almost every day. I miss them like crazy, but they know I'm still happy, probably more so than ever before, so it's all good. And I know that their door is always open to me, not that I will ever need to use it, but just knowing they've got my back is a good feeling. Don't get me wrong, leaving home was terrifying, but I know I made the right choice, and I couldn't be happier."

I wonder if I ever considered leaving home. I know I planned to go to The Art Institute after high school, so I must have liked it here in Charlotte, but was I going to stay at home or find an apartment in the city? Was there a person involved in my future plans? Or was I planning to go it alone?

"You okay over there?" Evie asks, pulling me out of my head. The car is parked and I look up to see we're already at the mall.

"I'm just wondering if I was happy here. I mean I guess I was since I wasn't planning to go very far for college. But I wonder if I'd made plans after high school with any friends. Was I going to continue living at home? I wish I could remember."

Evie looks thoughtful. "That must be tough. I couldn't even imagine." She shakes her head as if to clear the thoughts from it. She looks over to me and smiles, "I think you'll get your answers. One way or another, I think you'll get them."

For some reason, her firm statement makes me believe her. She seems certain, and I decide that I'm going to borrow her confidence and believe I will get answers.

***

We've only been in two stores, and I already have six bags full of clothes. According to Evie, we haven't even put a dent in Trevor's credit limit yet, but we haven't hit the shoe store yet, so there's that.

We're sitting in the food court, munching on some bourbon chicken, a mall food court staple according to Evie, when she says she needs to go to Victoria's Secret.

"Yeah, I could use some new bras and panties, too," I say in response.

Evie giggles. "That's *not* why I'm going there."

I give her a puzzled expression, "Why then?"

"I feel like a whale and need some sexy nighties and shit to feel more desirable," she says simply, like that answer should have been obvious.

"But you're pregnant," I say obtusely.

She full out laughs now, drawing attention from neighboring tables. "Exactly! I swear my libido has gotten a million times worse since I got knocked up. I thought I was horny before? Man, pre-pregnant Evie has nothing on pregnant Evie."

"Huh." Interesting, I guess.

"You should get yourself somethin' sexy, too." I shoot my eyes up at her, and she winks.

"What's the point?" I ask, looking down again as I fiddle with the remaining rice on my plate.

"Every woman should have a little somethin' in their wardrobe that makes them feel sexy. Even if it's just a lacy bra and panty set."

"It's not like there's anyone to see them," I say to my plate.

"Are you a virgin, Ally?" Evie asks quietly after a moment, and with what sounds like wonder in her voice.

My eyes shoot up to hers again. "I don't know," I spit out.

Her eyes widen. "Oh my Lord. I didn't even think about that! You don't have anyone you can ask?"

"Yeah," I laugh. "Let me go ask Alex if I'm a virgin. I don't know my former self at all, but I'm pretty sure she wouldn't have shared *that* with her brother."

Evie rolls her eyes at me. "I meant a girlfriend or something. Boyfriend?"

I shake my head. "No. I know I had a boyfriend, Blake, but we broke up a year before the accident. Apparently it was bad, so I'm not sure I'd get anything out of him. My former best friend, Lucy, is MIA, and my brothers said I only ever hung out with them and the band outside of school. And I'm pretty sure I never shared my sex life with the band."

"Well, there are other ways you can find out," she offered.

"Like what?" I wonder as I sip my Sprite.

"A doctor can tell you if your hymen is broken," she says so matter-of-factly that I spit my Sprite out in a spray across the table. Lucky for her, it didn't reach her side. "Gross, Ally! Man, you've got to be a virgin considering how much you're blushing right now talking about this," she laughs.

I glare at her.

"But seriously, if you can't find your Lucy friend, maybe you can talk with a doctor. Surely they'd understand your situation given your history. You need to go for annual lady doctor appointments anyway, so it wouldn't alert your brothers at all."

"Honestly, I'm not even sure I want to know," I tell her. "On the one hand, I want to know everything. On the other hand, I've been given a clean slate. Not too many people get that."

"But what if there's somethin' worth remembering? *Someone* worth remembering?" she questions.

"Then where has he been all this time?" I ponder.

I think about the other day on the couch with Chase and wish he could be that person to me. But that would be so complicated. I doubt we could ever be together like that. Not if my brothers had anything to say about it. I don't know them well, but I get the impression that they're super protective of me, even more so I'd guess since having me back. And while Chase is their friend, their brother, I'm still their little sister, and I have a feeling that would trump anything else.

# Chapter Nine

Chase and I have shared stolen moments almost every day since that day on the couch. It's only when he knows my brothers aren't home. If I stop and think about it too much, I'll wonder too much about keeping our budding relationship a secret. Because that's what it is and what seems to be happening, even if we haven't defined it yet.

We mostly hang out in the living room or the man room watching TV, like we're doing tonight, but sometimes he'll play his guitar and make notes in his notebook while I read my school books. Those times, I don't really get any reading done because I love watching the expressions play on his face as he concentrates, and I love hearing him play. I could never get tired of it.

Last night, he kissed me.

*We're laying on the couch together. This is the first time we have ever laid together; usually we just sit next to each other, and sometimes I will curl into his side like that first time we hung out. My back is to his front, and his arms are wrapped tightly around me. My heart is racing the entire time, and I have tingles all over. I am so nervous being here with him like this, but it feels so right at the same time. Like I belong here in his arms.*

*One of the* Transformers *movies is on the TV. I can't tell you which one, or what the plot is. But I can tell you what Chase is wearing, even though he's tucked behind me – blue jeans and a plain white t-shirt – he makes even the simplest attire hot. And what he smells like – pine and Polo Sport – I asked. And what his body feels like against mine – strong, solid, and safe.*

*After the movie is over and the credits are rolling, Chase nudges me. I look over my shoulder at him.*

*"What's up, baby girl?" he asks as he stares into my eyes.*

*"What do you mean?" I know he can tell I'm nervous; I swear I'm shaking on the inside like a cold, wet Chihuahua.*

*"You're so quiet," he says.*

"The movie was on."

"That doesn't usually stop you from talking." He's right. The past few days he could barely shut me up.

I shrug my shoulders.

He flips me so quickly, I'm not really sure what happened. I am now on my other side, facing him, and he is looking straight at my face. Now I feel more nervous than before. "What is it, baby girl?" he asks again.

I sigh, trying to find my courage. He's not going to let this go. "I like this," I say, gesturing at the smidgen of space between us.

A wide grin lights up his face. "I like this, too."

I smile shyly. "And I like you."

He runs his loose hand up and down my arm in a soothing gesture, as if he can feel my inner wet Chihuahua and is trying to calm her down. He doesn't realize it, but his touch is having the opposite effect. It is making my pulse race even more.

"I like you, too." He finally says.

I am mesmerized by his beautiful blues, and by the fact that this beautiful man likes me. He actually likes me. I don't realize I am smiling like a kid in a candy store until I see my smile reflected in his own.

"God, you're beautiful," he says quietly, then he leans forward and swiftly kisses me. His free hand goes up to my head, tangling in my hair and holding me close. His tongue licks the seam of my lips until I open my mouth to him. It's intense. Amazing. Hungry. This is the most amazing first kiss ever, and when he finally pulls away, both of us are panting. I can't help but want more.

Chase stares into my eyes for a beat, apparently as stunned as I am by what just happened. Then he pulls away from me. "I'm so sorry, Ally."

"What? Why?" I'm confused. I know this isn't ideal because we are sneaking around behind my brothers' backs and all, but why is he sorry?

He shakes his head, "I shouldn't have done that."

"Yes, you should have," I argue.

"No, Ally. It's not right. You're not in the right head space for something like that."

What? He doesn't think I am in the right head space? I'll show him I'm in the right head space. I lean forward, eliminating the gap between us, and kiss him. I kiss him with the same urgency and passion with which he just kissed me. This time it's my hand in his hair, pulling him closer. He groans, yes, groans, and deepens the kiss.

*I swear I could die tomorrow, and I would die happy.*

"What are you thinking about, gorgeous?" Chase asks me from the end of the couch, where my feet are resting in his lap.

"Nothing, handsome." I smile at him, and he smiles back. Yeah, I may be taking a detour from finding my old self, but at least it will be one hell of a ride.

# Chapter Ten

I'm eventually able to locate Lucy with Alex's help. With social media being as popular as it is, it shouldn't have been as difficult as it was, but considering I didn't have any accounts, and Alex had to delete his personal pages after their band reached stardom, we had to reach out to some of our old classmates the old-fashioned way to see who was still connected with her. And selecting which people we could contact who wouldn't go all fangirl or fanboy on him was not easy.

Unfortunately, Lucy is in California. I do have her phone number, but I was hoping for a face to face conversation. It's too easy to tell half-truths and flat-out lie when you're not looking into a person's eyes. I hate that I don't know who I can trust. And the fact that Lucy disappeared while I was in the hospital rubs me the wrong way.

I pick up the picture of Lucy and me that I had pulled from my bulletin board earlier today. We have our arms wrapped around each other's shoulders and big cheesy grins facing the camera. We're in our bathing suits, and it looks like we're at a beach. I remember Trevor saying something about our parents renting out a lake house occasionally, so maybe that's where we were.

At quick glance, Lucy and I could almost pass as sisters. We have the same sandy blonde hair and almost identical blue eyes. My tan is a little deeper than hers, at least in the picture. She's probably tanner than me now considering she's been in California the past year. It looks like she's a little bit taller than me, but we're both hunched over, so it's hard to tell.

I suck it up and dial her number. The line rings three times before someone picks up.

"Hello?"

"Is this Lucy?" I ask.

"A-Ally?" she answers back, sounding stunned.

"Yeah, it's me," I respond lamely, twirling the phone cord around my finger as I lean back in my father's old leather desk chair. I commandeered his office for this reconnaissance mission. Well, it wasn't really all that theatrical, I just wanted some privacy.

"Wow. I sure didn't expect to hear your voice." She doesn't sound displeased, just honestly surprised.

"Did I catch you at a bad time?" I ask, stalling.

"No, not at all. I just got in from a run a few minutes ago." I vaguely remember Alex pointing her out on the track team when we were looking at our yearbook a few days ago.

"I'm sorry to call out of the blue like this," I start.

"It's okay, Ally. It's really good to hear your voice. I heard you were out of the coma, but also I heard you had amnesia, so I didn't really know what to do."

"Yeah," I say. "I don't remember anything. My brothers told me about you, though. I know we were best friends, before the accident I guess."

"We were," she confirms, but doesn't say anything else. This is about as awkward as I thought it would be.

"I'm just trying to piece together some things," I continue, cutting to the chase. "I'm hoping you can help fill in some of the gaps."

"Sure, I'll try to do anything to help," she offers.

"Thanks," I say. "I'm not really sure where to start, but I guess I should ask, how are you? Are you doing okay?"

She sighs. "Yeah, I'm okay. College is good. I'm in California now, Stanford, which I guess you know since you're calling me and all. I stay in the dorms, but I live with my aunt in San Francisco on breaks and stuff."

"That's good," I say.

"Yeah, I like it here. Just started dating a guy; he's real sweet."

"That's great," I say, and mean it.

"So what can I help you out with?" she asks. "I bet you just have tons of questions if you can't remember anything."

"I do," I nod, even though she can't see me. "I was wondering if you can tell me anything about my relationship with Blake."

"Blake? Why?" she spits out. I guess I'm not all that surprised that this question has stunned her, considering what everyone has been telling me about our breakup.

"My brothers couldn't tell me much about our breakup. Only that it was bad. And I'm not sure I should call him and ask. I'm just trying to piece things together, and I'm kind of curious about other things, too."

"What other things?" she asked skeptically.

"Like if we ever slept together," I say quietly.

"You didn't sleep with Blake," she says quickly.

"Okay," it comes out like a question.

"Your brothers are right. Your breakup with Blake was bad. He really hurt you, Ally. I don't know all the details because you never wanted to talk about it. But I know he screwed around on you *because* you wouldn't sleep with him."

That is pretty bad. I can only imagine how much it must have hurt to have my boyfriend of two years cheat on me. "I didn't tell you anything else?"

"No," she says simply.

"Weren't we close?" I question.

"Honestly?"

"Please," I beg. "I need the truth. I feel like my brothers sugarcoat some of the things that they tell me to protect me, but I need to know the truth."

"We kind of grew apart junior year. It wasn't really intentional or either of our faults. Or maybe it was both of our faults, I don't know. I mean, we still talked and all, but we didn't hang out as much. You were always with Blake or the band, and I was focused on school."

"Is that why you didn't stay at the hospital?" I ask. "Alex said you were there for a couple days and then disappeared." Now is as good a time as any to get clarification on the doubts I have about Lucy's loyalty to me back then.

"I bet he did. Alex is so dramatic. Some things obviously never change," she huffs out, not even bothering to hide her frustration with my brother. *Interesting.* "I stayed at the hospital as long as I could. I was so worried about you and upset about your parents; I didn't want to leave. No amount of distance between you and me could have changed that, Ally. I promise you that."

"So what happened?" By now I've completely wrapped my hand in the long phone cord and begin the process of untangling it since my fingertips have turned purple.

"My parents," she grounds out. It's been a long time, but you can tell she's still bitter about it. "You know how they are. Well, I guess you don't know how they are, but you did. They were ridiculous. I swear they didn't even want a kid. They just wanted to keep up with appearances. Successful doctor? Check! Trophy wife? Check! Smart daughter? Check! Right after graduation, I was shipped off to live with my aunt in California. They chased me down at the hospital to get me on the plane. I didn't want to go. I didn't want to leave you. But I had no choice."

If she's telling the truth, it makes sense. I see no reason why she would lie about that. Plus, she seems to have the perfect amount of bitterness towards her parents in her voice. "I'm sorry they did that to you."

"Well, I'm sorry I wasn't there for you," she says, and again I believe her. There's just something about Lucy that's comforting. Kind of like Chase. I guess inside I can tell that these people were close to me in my previous life.

"It's okay, it's not like I would have noticed, I guess."

She laughs lightly, "I guess."

"Um," I begin. "Was I seeing anyone? I mean, after Blake and before the accident?"

"I don't know," she says sadly. "Like I said, we weren't too close at the time. There were a few times when we talked on the phone, and it seemed like you were hushing someone in the background, but when I'd ask you about it, you'd just say it was nothing or there was no one there."

"Do you think I was sneaking around with someone?" I sit up straight in my chair. Now we're getting somewhere.

"I can't see how that would've been possible." I instantly deflate. "I mean, you spent practically every waking moment with your brothers and the band. When you weren't at school, you were in the garage with them while they practiced, or at their shows."

This sounds remarkably like my current relationship with Chase. If it's even a relationship. I sure hope it is, but it's kind of hard to define something that's a secret. Is this not my first secret relationship? What type of person would that make me?

"But my behavior was suspicious enough for you to point it out," I state.

"Yeah, I guess. We didn't talk much senior year, but a few of the times we did, it really did seem like you were holding something back. I just didn't know what it was and was so consumed with my own stuff that I didn't think to ask."

"Well, I guess if it was a guy, it's not really worth figuring it out," I decide, leaning back in the chair again.

"Why do you say that?" she asks, genuinely curious.

"If I was in a relationship with a guy before the accident, where is he now? Obviously it couldn't have been all sunshine and rainbows if he's not around anymore. What kind of guy abandons his girl when she's in a coma? And doesn't even come to see me after?" I silently wonder if this is something I can just let go of.

"Well, I'm sure your brothers have kept a pretty close watch on you. If you were hiding a relationship back then, maybe he hasn't had an opening to say something without your brothers around. Maybe he doesn't know how to approach you, or he doesn't think you'd believe him since you don't remember. Or maybe he's away at school."

I get what she's saying, and it's totally valid, but I still don't know what to think about all this. "I guess there's a lot to consider."

"If it's any consolation, you were really happy, Al."

This gets my attention. "What do you mean?"

"Near the end of senior year, you were really happy. I'm not sure I had ever seen you so happy. After everything happened with Blake, you were in a pretty dark place. The rest of junior year was pretty bad for you. I mean nobody talked smack about it because they knew Alex would have gone ape shit, but you were really sad. By the end of senior year, it was like you did a complete one-eighty. You were happy, glowing even."

I ponder that for a minute. Is it possible that just spending time with the band made that big a difference in my life? I have fun with them now, I imagine back when I actually knew them I had even more fun. But there's no way I can answer that question now. It makes me think of Chase again, he makes me happy. Really happy. Do I glow? Am I glowing?

"Can I throw in my two cents?" Lucy asks, interrupting my musings.

"Please, I'm driving myself crazy here. I could use some insight that isn't from one of the chapters of 'Life According to Alex.'"

Lucy laughs. "You poor thing. I know you don't really know me anymore, but if you ever need some girl talk, please promise you'll call me. Hanging out with all that testosterone can't be healthy."

"I will, thanks, Lucy." It would do me good to have another girl friend besides Evie, and Lucy seems like the perfect candidate, even if it is long distance.

"You're welcome. But now for my two cents. You were really happy, Al. I can tell you're pretty much ready to brush that off, but my advice is not to. Whether it was some*thing* or some*one*, I think you owe it to yourself to figure out what it was. Maybe there's a reason it isn't present in your life right now, or maybe it's present and you just don't realize it." I immediately think of Chase. I'm not sure why, other than the fact that I can't seem to *not* think about him. And because he makes me happy. Would discovering someone in my past rock that boat?

"I've pretty much exhausted my resources for memories. I'm not really sure where else to go to for information." I take a frustrated spin in the office chair, curling myself up in the stupid phone cord in the process. Why the heck does this phone have a cord anyway? Doesn't everyone have cordless phones? Or cell phones?

"What about the band?" she offers. "That's who you spent most of your time with. Surely they would have picked up on something."

"But wouldn't Trevor or Alex have told me by now?" Although they did neglect to tell me I had a boyfriend at first.

"Not necessarily. Not if they weren't specifically trying to recall it. I mean, if you were hiding something from me, chances are you were hiding it from them even more." She's got a point.

"So what good would talking to them do?" I press, getting frustrated with the whole situation.

"Tell them specifically what you're looking for, see if they remember anything slight or suspicious. Ask all the guys, maybe Joey or Chase caught something. It won't hurt to ask," she reminds me. I could ask Chase. He said I could talk to him about anything. But my little research project has the potential to hurt whatever it is Chase and me are building. What if I did have a boyfriend before the accident? And what if there *is* a valid reason he is currently absent?

"Or it could open up a can of worms," I groan.

"Why do you say that?" she asks.

"What if it throws a complete curveball into my life? What if it's something bad?

"That wasn't you, Al. You didn't have it in you to get involved in something bad. There's no way you could have hidden something bad anyway. You're way too transparent, and you would have had guilt written all over your face. Plus, like I said, you were happy. Not nervous or worried, and if you were hiding something negative, I'm sure you would have been jittery as hell. It might throw a curveball, I'm sure any memory or revelation would at this point, but I don't think it was something negative."

Well, that's a relief, I guess. At least *she* seems confident.

"Seriously, thanks, Lucy. I know this call was unexpected and now I've taken up a big chunk of your time. I really appreciate that you've talked to me."

"I'm glad we had the chance to talk. I've missed you a lot, Ally."

"I'm glad we spoke, too. Can we talk again soon?" I add. I can't say that I miss her, for obvious reasons, but I'm being honest when I say I'd like to talk to her again.

"Definitely, you don't even have to ask. Call me again soon, or text me. This is my cell. Especially if you figure anything out."

"I will," I promise. "Bye Lucy."

"Bye, Ally."

I hang up the phone and spin around in the desk chair a few more times as I think. What could I have been hiding? Lucy said I was transparent, so how could I have gotten away with hiding something in the first place? Especially if it was some kind of relationship. But then again, I'm hiding whatever it is between me and Chase now. Even though it's almost completely innocent at this point, except for that kiss. Maybe I'm better at hiding things than everyone thinks.

It just doesn't make sense. But she's right, if anyone would know anything, it's the band. They had to have unknowingly seen or heard something. I could ask Chase, but I don't know how he'd react to hearing that I might have been in a relationship before the accident. Where would that leave us now? I don't remember this other person I may or may not have been with, but I absolutely remember my recent times with Chase.

Every moment I spend with him is more amazing than the last. I really would like to see how things play out with him, but is that fair? What if we start something and I regain my memories of someone else? Is it appropriate for me to start something with Chase without disclosing my concerns about what may or may not have happened the year before the accident?

Lucy is right, I might find answers with the band. But I know I have to talk to Chase first. I have to be completely honest with him if I want a relationship to develop, and I can't blindside him in front of all the other guys. I need to get him alone.

# Chapter Eleven

Trevor and Alex are both home tonight, so I text Chase to let him know I want to meet him at his apartment. I know it's risky, doing this while my brothers are home, but I can't wait another minute. I want answers.

"Hey, baby girl," Chase croons as I slip in the side door to the garage. I'm surprised to see him downstairs in the band's practice space, rather than waiting for me upstairs in his apartment. We can easily be caught down here if my brothers were to come by for their instruments or a visit.

I give him a shy smile, "Hey, Chase."

He sets his acoustic guitar on the couch beside him and stands. "To what do I owe the pleasure of this clandestine meeting?" he asks as he struts towards me.

God, he's gorgeous. I could look into his eyes all day long and not get tired of it. Then there's the way he walks and the way he talks. I could get lost in him. I want to get lost *with* him.

"Ally," he says, snapping his fingers in front of my face.

I startle and shake my thoughts of his bottomless blue eyes from my head. "I wanted to ask you something," I tell him. "Can we go upstairs?"

"You wanna go upstairs?" he smirks and wriggles his eyebrows.

I roll my eyes and laugh. "Yes, but not for the reasons I'm sure you're thinking." He visibly deflates. "At least not right away." I add, boldly running my fingertips down his toned bicep. I throw in a wink, and he perks back up. "I just don't want my brothers to walk in."

"You know it'll be a lot worse if they walk in and we're upstairs, right?"

"Well, I'm not planning on them walking in, and if they do, I'll hide in your closet or something."

"My closet is in my bedroom," he says, scratching his chin as though he's deep in thought. "I kind of like the idea of you in my bedroom." He grins mischievously again and tingles erupt throughout my entire body.

"Head out of the gutter, Baker," I finally say.

He smiles to let me know he's teasing me. "Come on," he says as he grabs my hand and leads me up the stairs to his apartment.

I haven't been up here before. It's really nice. It's set up like a studio, with everything out in the open except for the bathroom and what I guess is a closet. There's a small kitchenette when you first walk in, complete with a breakfast bar and two stools. To the left there is a seating area with a leather couch, entertainment center, and small coffee table. These boys and their leather furniture. I try to ignore his large bed in the farthest corner of the space, but recall him just mentioning his bedroom. I thought for sure that meant a separate space. I take a seat on the couch and Chase sits beside me, never releasing my hand.

"What's going on, baby girl? You seem so serious." Nervous is more like it, but Chase was probably just being polite.

"I thought you said you had a bedroom?" I ask, trying to shake the nerves out.

He smirks again, "This whole place is my bedroom."

I roll my eyes, "On that note..." I take a deep breath. "I wanted to talk to you about some things."

"So you said," he says, referring to my earlier texts I'm sure. I had never texted him before, never really needed to. He always kind of showed up before I could think even think about it.

I look into his eyes again, which are now filled with concern. "I don't think it's anything bad," I say, trying to assure him.

"That's good," he says, but he still doesn't relax his expression.

"I spoke with Lucy today," I start. I haven't spoken to Chase much about wanting to find the missing pieces of my life. I tend to want to live in the now when I'm with him and he encourages that. He's so understanding about everything, and his opinions are so fresh. He doesn't worry about coddling me, he just tells it like it is, and he does it in a way that's not offensive or hurtful. I can tell he genuinely cares. And I worry that he may not like the idea of me digging into my past and not just letting things happen naturally.

"That's good. What did you talk about?"

"Just stuff," I say, looking down at my lap. What was I thinking? How can I mention a possible hidden fling from my past to my current hidden fling? Ugh. How messed up am I? Two hidden flings?

Chase puts his finger under my chin and lifts my head to face him. "What is it, baby girl? You know you can tell me anything."

I nod because, yes, I do know that. I take a deep breath and let it all out in a quick exhale. "Lucy seems to think I might have been seeing someone before the accident."

I watch the emotions flash across his face. Shock, fear, was that relief?

"What makes you think that?" he asks calmly.

I look at him for a moment before I respond. "She didn't know for sure, she just mentioned some peculiar behaviors. Said I was pretty transparent and that it seemed like I was hiding something, or some*one*. She heard voices when I was on the phone with her sometimes, but I'd just tell her it was nothing."

He seems to consider this, then asks, "What did you want to ask me?"

Right. I did want to ask him something. "I was wondering if maybe you remembered anything from the time I used to hang out with you guys. Maybe you saw or heard something that might help me figure out what I was up to?"

He stands up and begins to pace, running his hands through his hair over and over again, and mumbling to himself. I can't make out what he's saying, but his whole reaction strikes me as a bit odd. I didn't think he'd love the idea of there being someone in my life before when we've got something building between us now, but I didn't expect this. It seems like he's close to losing it, and he's always been so calm and collected.

"Chase?" He pauses and looks over to me. I can't even explain the look on his face. He looks absolutely torn. Oh my God, does he know something? "Do you know something?"

He continues to stare at me as more of the same emotions wash over his face, only this time there is sadness as well. "I," he starts. Then he shakes his head and turns away from me to resume pacing.

I get up from my place on the couch and boldly approach him. I wrap my arms around his waist and rest my cheek against his back. He immediately stops his forward motion and tenses up, but then relaxes and puts his hands over mine. "It's okay, Chase. Whatever it is, it's okay."

He takes a deep breath, then says "I'm sorry, Ally, but I don't know anything."

Huh. Well, that I didn't expect. Based off his reaction alone I thought he knew something. But maybe it was just the thought of something coming between us that upset him. I do my best to reassure him.

"Chase, whatever it is, whatever happened before, I want you to know that I care about you a lot. I like what we've got going here, and I don't want anything to change that. Things from the past might come up, and it might make me, or us, question things, but I'm happy here, now, with you. I want to see what this is."

He sighs and squeezes my hands, then he turns around. Looking into my eyes, he frames my face with his hands. "You don't know how good it is to hear you say that, baby girl." He leans forward and gives me a brief, soft kiss. "I care about you a lot, too. I want us to have a real shot, so I'm being very careful here. I don't want to make anyone upset, and you've been through a lot, so I don't want to push you before you're ready. But just know that I feel the same way you do, I care about you so much. I don't want to lose you. I can't lose you."

I lay my head against his chest and smile. This man completely disarms me. He knows all the right things to say, all the time. It's almost too good to be true, but he's right here in front of me. I can see him and feel him, so I know he's real. When he wraps his arms around me and kisses the top of my head, I melt.

"I'm going to ask the guys about it, too. Just to see if they remember anything." I feel him stiffen under me. "I promise it's not going to change anything between us."

He pulls back and looks me in the eyes, his face completely serious. "I'm not sure that's a good idea."

"What? Why?"

"Just think about it, Al. If you didn't tell anyone before, maybe there was a reason."

I think about it, and he's right. It was the same concern I had when I talked to Lucy. I didn't want to create any unnecessary trouble. Things are going well with me and my brothers, and with me and Chase. Why rock the boat?

"You're right," I rest my head on his chest. "If it's meant to be revealed, it will be."

He exhales, and I feel his body lose its tension. He wraps his arms around me again and holds me close. "I don't want to lose you, baby girl."

I laugh, he's so silly. As if he'd lose me. "I'm not going anywhere," I promise him. He sighs and his grip tightens, as if he's afraid if he lets go of me, I'm going to float away or something.

"I hope not," he whispers.

We spend the rest of the evening curled up together on his couch, but something is off. Chase doesn't kiss me or even really touch me. He just holds me as close as he can, my head tucked under his chin, like he really is afraid I am going to disappear.

Around midnight, I finally sneak back into my house, and I make it all the way to my room without bumping into my brothers.

As I lay in my bed, I think about the entire scene with Chase. He just wasn't himself, and I don't know what I make of it. He seemed... scared. When I said goodnight, he held me so close and kept telling me he didn't want to lose me.

Maybe it has something to do with the accident. We were all close back then, so it could be that he felt he lost me back then, and now, the idea that there might be another man makes him feel like he could lose me now, in a completely different way than before. I wish there was some way I could reassure him that that's not the case. I only know him; I only want him. I can't imagine feeling any differently.

I finally fall asleep to dreams of the color blue.

# Chapter Twelve

School has started and I'm in seventh heaven. I love my classes, and I'm really good at it, too. I'm not sure if it's innate talent, or if it's because I've already read all my books, but I'm only two weeks in and already getting complimented left and right by my instructors on my techniques. I've even made friends with a couple of my classmates. It's nice having people outside of the band to talk to and commiserate with.

Things between Chase and me are... complicated. It's been a few weeks since we had our talk in his apartment, and since then, he has been a little distant. I guess a part of him might be worried about the skeletons that may be lurking in my closet, but I thought he would have gotten over it by now. I've told him time and time again that I'm only interested in him now, and that should be what matters. I know the distance doesn't help either. It was already hard enough spending time together in secret, but now I'm in classes five days a week and studying the rest of the time, and he's involved in the prep for the new album and upcoming tour. It's even more difficult for us to find time together.

Part of me still wonders if I should confront my brothers and Joey to see if they have any idea of what I was up to before the accident. After the talk with Chase, I kind of let it go, happy to live in the now with him and returning to my original theory of whoever or whatever it was not being important enough if they or it could so easily disappear from my life. But it's always going to be that niggling thought in the back of my mind, and maybe in the back of Chase's as well. Maybe finding out some answers and putting it to bed once and for all will remove the strain on our relationship and allow us to finally move forward and come out of hiding. I hate lying to my brothers. Even if it's just a lie of omission, it's still a lie, and it's not how I want to base our relationship.

I wish I could talk to Evie or Lucy about all this, but to do that and get a legitimate opinion from them, I'd have to reveal my relationship with Chase, and I'm not sure we're anywhere near ready to go public. Especially since we're in this limbo state.

Lucy already gave me her opinion on the pre-accident situation, so she'd probably only reiterate that anyway. We've spoken a few times since our first conversation, but I conveniently steered clear of the topic, and I guess she knew enough not to ask. And Evie is just way too close to the guys to talk to about Chase. She'd probably tell Joey, who would in turn tell my brothers. When it came to Trevor and Alex, it had to come from me.

There's really only one thing left for me to do to try to get to the bottom of this once and for all. I have to talk to the guys. I want me and Chase to be able to move forward. No matter what Dr. Moody or anyone else thinks about me delving into my past, I can't not push this. I want to know that I did everything I could to figure it out so that I will no longer be bothered by the questions in my mind. Nearly every other moment of my life can be explained in some way by someone. The things Lucy said cannot. This is something I need to know. And I want to find out and then let it all go. I just hope it doesn't upset Chase.

*\*\**

I'm pacing the entrance to the man room, nervous as hell. I had slept on my thoughts from the previous day and decided that I had to talk to the band. I wasted no time calling a band meeting, which, needless to say brought some interesting reactions since I'm not technically *in* the band.

The guys should be here any minute, and I have no idea how I'm going to broach the subject. I'm forcing myself to think positively. Everyone has been nothing but supportive of me, and I can't imagine this will be any different. But I'm still worried about Chase. I hope he understands that I have to know, *why* I have to know.

I pull my cell phone out of my pocket when I hear a beep indicating a text. It's Lucy. *It'll be fine, you'll do great. Stop worrying.* I had sent her a text this morning when I woke up, letting her know I was finally going to talk to them. She encouraged me, and I told her to think positive thoughts at noon, when the guys agreed to take a break from their studio time to meet with me.

I felt awful interrupting their time at the studio because I know they're trying to get the finishing touches done on the album before they leave for tour in a couple months. The album is supposed to drop in a month, and hopefully the timing will boost ticket sales for their shows.

*Thanks,* I text back to Lucy. There's little question in my mind as to whether or not she had been my best friend before. She obviously knew me well enough to know I'd need some encouragement right about now.

As I'm tucking my phone back into my pocket, the guys arrive. They look exhausted after all the work they've been doing at the studio, and again I'm thankful they agreed to meet with me anyway.

They grab assorted beverages from the kitchen – Gatorade, bottled water, and soda – and make their way into the man room. Alex and Joey sit on the sofa, Trevor sits on the recliner, and Chase gestures for me to sit in the last remaining seat, a plain black arm chair, but I shake my head and motion for him to sit. I'm too nervous to sit still.

"So what's going on, kid?" Trevor asks.

Blunt and straightforward, I tell myself. I take a deep breath in and let it out. "Well, you guys know I've been trying to put together pieces of my past." I pause for a moment while they nod their understanding. "The year before the accident seems to be the biggest blank."

Out of the corner of my eye, I swear I see Chase stiffen, but when I look over at him, he's completely composed. I haven't seen him in a few days, and I want nothing other than to crawl into his lap and have him hold me tight. I worry that my pursuit of this is going to hurt him, but he just smiles softly at me.

Bringing myself back to focus, I continue. "You guys know I've been in contact with Lucy." They all nod so I continue. "She got me thinking about what happened after I broke up with Blake. I mean, I know I hung out with you all a lot after that, but that's all I really know. Lucy said she and I kind of grew apart that year because she was focusing on school and prepping for college, and I spent most of my time with the band. So she didn't really have any insight for me."

"Yeah," Trevor says. "You hung out in the garage with us while we practiced and went to our gigs with us." The rest of the group nods their agreement. "I don't think you really did anything else."

Oh, how I wish that was the case. Now for the hard part.

"Lucy mentioned something the first time we spoke." I looked over at Chase and hoped my eyes expressed my apology. "She said that a few times when she talked to me on the phone, it sounded like I was with someone, that I was hushing them or something. But when she would ask me about it I just kind of brushed it off and said it was no one or nothing. She kind of made it sound like I might have been sneaking around or something."

"What do you mean?" Trevor asks, as he leans forward in his seat.

"I don't really know. That's why I asked you guys to meet with me. I was hoping that maybe since I spent so much time with you all, that maybe you saw something that you didn't think was anything at the time. Maybe with this new information from Lucy, it will mean something?"

"I really don't remember anything that stands out, Ally."

"I figured you would have said something if you did, Trev. But the thing is, if I was sneaking around, then it probably wouldn't have stood out, you know?" I wring my hands in front of me, hoping one of them has a break through.

Trevor nods his understanding. "After school you'd come home, do any homework you didn't finish in study hall, and then come out to the garage. We'd go in for dinner, or out, and then head back out to the garage. And when mom called you inside, you went. I really can't think of any gaps of time that are unaccounted for."

Joey chimes in next. "I can't think of anything either, girl. Sorry."

I nod. "It's okay. I knew it was a long shot."

I look over to Chase, he's hunched over, his elbows on his knees and his head in his hands. Alex is glaring in Chase's direction. Does Chase know something? Does Alex?

"Chase?" I ask, drawing Trevor's and Joey's attention to him as well. He picks up his head and looks at me, obvious pain is displayed all over his face. Then he glances at Alex's harsh stare, then over to Trevor's concerned face, before finally landing on Joey's curious one.

He lets out a sigh and shakes his head. "I'm so sorry, Ally."

# Part Two
# Chase

# Chapter Thirteen

*One year before the accident*

"I think that's good for tonight, guys," Trevor says as he wipes the sweat off his forehead with his arm. We've been practicing in his parents' garage for three hours already. Even with the A/C Mr. Monroe installed and the fans we added, it's still hot.

"Yeah, mom and dad have been riding my ass for staying out here so late this past week," Alex adds. He's the only one of us still in school, junior year of high school. Joey should have been, too, but he dropped out a year before. Shit like that happened when you didn't have parents that gave a shit about you, not that I could talk. I didn't have parents who gave a shit, but I still finished school. That was mainly thanks to all the time I spent at Trevor's house growing up, Mr. and Mrs. Monroe treated me like their fourth child. They would have done the same with Joey, but he didn't let them. He was a bit of a loner, and while he loved the family and all of us, he kept his attachments limited to his best friend, Alex.

I pack up my guitar and set it next to Trevor's bass in the corner. Joey tucks his sticks into his back pocket, and together we all walk out the side door to the driveway. We say our goodbyes, and I offer Joey a ride home, which he declines like always. I know it's because he's not in a rush to get there. Trevor and Alex head into the house, and I go to my car, which is parked in the street.

"Shit. I don't have my keys," I say to myself.

I turn around and head back up the driveway. I go to enter the code in the keypad lock on the garage door, but pause when I hear what sounds like sniffling. I look around but I don't see anyone, and it's gone quiet again, so I enter the code in the pad and turn the knob. My keys are just where I thought I'd left them, on the side table next to the couch.

Mr. and Mrs. Monroe were pretty cool for setting this place up for us, complete with couches, carpet, acoustic ceilings, central air, cable, a small bathroom, and a mini-fridge. It was like an apartment. Hell, Joey and I've even slept in there a few times when we didn't want to go home. Trevor, Alex, and Ally hit the parent lottery with those two, and they knew it.

I grab my keys and lock back up. As I'm walking back down the driveway, I hear the sniffle again, this time followed by a sob. Now I know I'm not imagining things. I quickly turn and walk back towards the house. I step in between the house and the garage and head for the backyard. The only person I can think of who would be out here is Ally, and I hope to hell nothing is wrong and she's okay.

I look around the yard, taking in her usual favorite places. She's not on the tire swing, or on the bench in her mother's garden. She's not sitting on the deck either. I scan the grass, but she's nowhere to be found.

"Ally?" I call out in a loud whisper. I hear another sniffle and turn around. There, sitting on the ground with her back pressed up against the side of the garage is Ally. She has her knees pulled up to her chest and her forehead resting on them. Her arms are wrapped tightly around her legs.

I step over to her and squat down. "Ally, are you okay?" Stupid question to ask a crying girl, I know, but I'm a guy. We don't always know better.

"I'm fine, just leave me alone, Chase." She says as she sniffles, but it's muffled since she's talking into her lap.

"You know I can't do that, kid."

She picks her head up so fast I startle and fall back onto my ass. "I'm not a fucking kid!" she yells.

I frown when I see the makeup smudged on her face and smell the alcohol on her breath. "Have you been drinking? Did someone do something to you?" I ask, assuming the absolute worst.

She glares at me before tucking her head back on her knees. "Just go away."

I prop myself back up and onto my knees so I have a little more stability in case she erupts again. "Ally, you know I'm not going to do that. Not without at least letting your brothers or your parents know you're out here."

"I didn't ask for you to come save me, Chase." Her voice breaks mid-sentence.

"What happened, Al?" I try softly. I bet it was her douchebag boyfriend. Little shit was never good enough for her.

"Nothing," she snaps. "Just go on and go. And if you tell my parents or my brothers I'm out here, I will go in that garage and break your damn guitar."

Well, that's hitting a little below the belt. Threatening assault on a musician's instrument was like insulting a momma's boy's mother. But I'm not going to get mad, not when she's obviously been through something tonight.

"I won't tell on you," I say soothingly, like I'm dealing with a wounded, scared animal. I guess in a sense I am. "Just talk to me? I swear whatever you say will be in complete confidence."

After a few minutes, she picks her head up and looks at me, then nods.

"Why don't we go sit in the garage, let you get some water and get cleaned up, okay?" I stand up slowly, afraid if I move too quickly I might startle her. I put my hand out to pull her up, and she takes it. She doesn't let go as she follows me to the garage. I punch in the code and open the door. "Ladies first," I say, sweeping my hand in front of us. Corny, I know.

She lets go of my hand and walks in, setting her purse on the side table where my keys had just been. Thank God I left them behind, who knows how long she would have been out there by herself if I hadn't found her. I flip on the light and she quickly reaches over to turn it back off.

"I don't want to attract any attention from my family," she tells me, and I nod. "I'm just going to use the restroom," she says quietly as she hurries over to the small bathroom.

I go to the fridge and pull out a couple bottles of water, then sit down on the couch. I have no idea what I'm doing here. I'm not an emotional guy, at all. Yeah, I have feelings just like anyone else, but girl problems? Not my area of expertise. I don't know what to do with a crying woman or girl rather. Ally is sixteen, almost seventeen. Teenage girl problems? Even worse.

Ally comes out of the bathroom a moment later with what seems like a little more pep in her step. "I can't believe you didn't tell me I looked like a raccoon," she jokes as she sits on the couch beside me.

"You want to tell me why you looked like a raccoon?" I ask. I know what she's doing, trying to get me to forget I just found her crying on the side of her house at eleven o'clock at night. Well, I'm *not* going to forget, and she *is* going to tell me what has her so upset.

"Blake and I broke up last week," she says simply.

Well, I kind of figured that much. "What did that little asswipe do to you?"

"He didn't *do* anything," she spits out.

"What did he say?"

"Nothing that wasn't true." Her voice wavers and part of the armor she put on in the bathroom melts away.

"You know you can't believe anything he says. He's a tool; he doesn't know shit."

"He might not be the brightest guy, but *this* he knows." She sniffs again, and she's looking down so I can't see her eyes, but I bet she's crying again.

"What did he say, Al?" I rest my hand on her back and she jumps. "Did he fucking hit you?" I roar.

"What? No! God, no! He didn't lay a hand on me. I guess that's the problem." She laughs through her tears. "I wouldn't let him lay a hand on me. He said I was frigid. He called me frigid when I caught him cheating on me with some bimbo. We'd been together for nearly two years and never had sex. So he went and got it somewhere else." She lets out a big sob and starts shaking with her cries.

I put my arm around her shoulders and pull her into me, not knowing what else to do. I want to get up and drive to Blake's house and beat the shit out of him for hurting her, but instead, I just hold her tighter.

"Told you he was a tool," I say, and I think I hear her laugh a little. "You're not frigid, Ally. He just wasn't the right guy for you and deep down inside, you knew it."

"But we were together two years," she says. "If I knew he wasn't right for me, why were we still together?"

"Because you were comfortable? Shit, I don't know. I don't do relationships."

"Right," she scoffs. "You and my brother just have microwave relationships. Love 'em and leave 'em. Thirty seconds and their done."

I know that's what she thinks I do, sleep with random chicks and then blow them off. But that's not entirely true. Sure I've fooled around with a lot of girls. It's easy when you're a good-looking guy in a band. And yeah, I probably sound conceited for referring to myself as a good-looking guy, but it is what it is. I've been told I'm hot enough times that I believe it.

I don't know what makes me tell Ally my deepest, darkest secret. Maybe it's the look in her eyes, the look that tells me she really does believe that she's pathetic for not sleeping with her boyfriend of two years. Maybe it's the fact that I don't want her to feel so alone. Maybe I just want her to stop crying. Anyway, I don't know what it is, but I tell her.

"I'm a virgin, too, Al."

She lifts her head up and looks at me, then she laughs. "Yeah, right. Nice try, Chase."

Well, that's not how I saw this conversation going. "I'm serious," I tell her.

She shakes her head, "Chase, I appreciate what you're trying to do here. But you don't have to say that."

"It's the truth. I've fooled around with a lot of girls, but I've never slept with any of them." I look straight at her as I tell her this, willing her to see the truth in my eyes.

"You're not joking," she states as she looks into my eyes.

"No, I'm not."

"Why?" she asks.

"Why what?"

"What's your reason? For still being a virgin?"

Now, this, this I didn't want to talk about. I look down at my hands in my lap. "I just haven't met the right girl."

"You're lying," she says quietly. My eyes meet hers again. "That may be part of it, but it's not the whole truth." How can she read me like that? "I know what you guys deal with at shows and stuff. If there wasn't some serious reason stopping you from having sex, then you would've just done it already with one of your many groupies just to get it over with."

She was right, but did I want to tell her that? Not really. Was I going to anyway? Probably.

"You can tell me, Chase. If you want to. I'm a good listener, and maybe I will understand better than you think."

I highly doubt that. But it seems like talking is getting her out of the funk I found her in, so what the hell. "You know my home life is shit," I begin and she nods. "Well, after my dad left, I grew up watching my mother parade men in and out of her bedroom." I see her eyes widen before I continue. "Our house was the 'it' place for drugs, alcohol, and sex. No one ever messed with me directly, but the situation messed with me."

"I'm so sorry, Chase." She rests her hand on my knee in a gesture of reassurance. "I had no idea your home life was like that. I mean I knew it wasn't good, but I didn't know what went on."

"It's not like that anymore. My mom still drinks a lot and smokes pot, but the guys don't come around anymore. Probably stopped when I got bigger than all of them, and the drugs and alcohol finally took a toll on her appearance. Anyway, it all made me realize that I wanted better for myself than that. That's why I don't do drugs, get drunk, or sleep around. When I think about those things, I think back to those times, and it nearly makes me sick."

She smiles softly at me. "I think it's good that you took those experiences and made something positive out of them for yourself. That you want something better than that for yourself. A lot of people in those situations don't end up making good decisions."

"Thanks," I tell her, not knowing what else to say.

"Thanks for making me talk to you," she says as she leans back against the couch. "I feel a little better, and less defective."

"Could be the water, too," I say gesturing to the two empty bottles on the coffee table. She had finished mine as well. "Mind telling me while you smelled like a brewery?"

She closes her eyes and sighs. "I bumped into Blake and his new girl at a house party some friends from school were having. I got really upset, and I had a couple beers out of the keg. And some shots."

"Ally, I don't think I need to tell you that you shouldn't go to parties by yourself. Even if you know people there. You need the buddy system or something. Not to mention the fact that you were drinking. Anything could have happened, and your night could have ended up a lot worse than you just crying in the yard."

She had opened her eyes during my monologue, and when I look over at her, I see her chin quivering and tears in her eyes. Damn it. Now I upset her.

"Shit, I'm sorry, Ally. You're like a sister to me and I'd hate to see anything bad happen to you. There are too many assholes out there." She nodded, but a few tears broke free. I put my arm around her and pulled her into my side again.

"Look, if you ever need to talk, about anything at all, I'm here, okay? I won't go repeating everything you say back to your brothers. It'll just be between us. I want you to have someone you can count on to talk to and not judge."

"You'd be that person for me? Really?" she asks, meeting my eyes.

"Of course," I nod, never feeling more sure of anything.

She leans back down into my side. "So, we're like, friends?" she asks.

"Yeah. It's not that hard a concept to understand." I look at her like she's nuts. Why is this a big deal?

"I know, but you're Trevor's best friend. It's just weird that you're my friend now, too. Plus, you're like, old," she stifles a giggle.

"I'm only twenty-one," I laugh, giving her a noogie. "I'm not that old."

"Ouch, that hurts," she laughs. She tries to twist away but I've tightened my hold around her.

"Take it back," I tell her.

"Fine, you're not old! You're a spring chicken!"

"Really?" I laugh as I let her go. "Damn, your hair is a mess!" Some of her sandy blonde strands are pulled from her ponytail and going in all different directions from my noogie.

She shrugs and settles back down onto the couch. "Want to watch TV for a little bit? I don't want to go inside yet."

"Sure," I say grabbing the remote. We argue back and forth between *Storage Wars,* her favorite, and *Overhaulin',* my favorite. We end up flipping between both shows during the commercials before she eventually falls asleep, resting her head on the arm of the couch. She looks so peaceful, but I can't leave her out here all night alone, and I surely can't stay here with her either.

I wake her up gently and walk her to the front door of her house. "You gonna be okay?" I ask.

She smiles a genuine smile. "Yeah. Thanks for tonight, friend."

"You're welcome, friend."

She laughs and unlocks the front door. Once she's safely inside, I check my pocket for my keys and head for my car.

Chase Baker, friends with a girl. Who would have thunk it?

# Chapter Fourteen

Ally has started hanging out in the garage during band practices, and since the guys all know now that she broke up with Blake, they don't think or say much of her sudden reappearance. She used to hang out and watch the band practice all the time, she even named us. But once her and the douchebag started dating, she spent most of her time with him, only showing up to watch us play in the garage or at shows once in a while. We're all thrilled to have our number one fan back.

I've kept my word and haven't told the guys about the night I found her outside crying, so they don't know that we've started up a little friendship. We chat mainly through texts, deciding that if they catch us talking, they're likely to ask questions, which will lead back to that night.

It's a Wednesday, and we don't practice on Wednesdays because Joey has to work that night at the home improvement store. We all have jobs we work during the day, but that's their big stock night, so it's the one night a week he works evenings. We all usually use that night to do non-band things like dates, or when you're a Monroe, family night. I'm always invited to family night, but don't always attend since it's a constant reminder of how fucked up, and non-existent, my family is.

But tonight I'm going. Why? Because Ally asked me to.

**Ally:**     Are you coming tonight?

**Me:**     nah, u guys have fun.

**Ally:**     Please? We're playing Pictionary and the teams will be uneven. Plus, Alex can't draw for shit and I don't want to get stuck on his team.

**Me:**     arent u twins? if he cant draw, doesnt that mean u cant draw either? y would i want 2 b on ur team?

**Ally:**     We're not identical! Plus, twins don't share talent like they do genes.

**Me:**     i know, i was just messing with u.

- 145 -

**Ally:**    So you'll come?

**Me:**    yeah, if its cool with ur parents, i will b there.

**Ally:**    They invite you every week, of course it's cool with them! And do you realize that it takes me an extra minute to translate some of your texts?

She's always such a ballbuster.

**Me:**    omg.  r  u  serious?  wtf  smh rotflmao so sry

**Ally:**    ...

**Me:**    c u at 6.

**Ally:**    Bye, Chase.

**Me:**    l8r

I park my car in my usual spot at the curb and hustle up to the front door, it's five after and Mrs. Monroe, as sweet as she is, is a stickler for punctuality. I knock on the door and wait, pretty sure that I'm now going to get chided for two things when she opens the door.

Annnd she doesn't disappoint. Opening the door is an older version of Alex and Ally, well, more like Ally since she's a female and all, but the three of them share that same sandy blonde hair and blue eyes. "What have I told you about knocking? You're late, Chase."

She always tells me to come right in, and as much as they make me feel like a part of their family, it still feels weird just walking into their home. "Hi, Mrs. Monroe," I say as I walk past her into the house. I give her a quick kiss on the cheek and she tells me to go on into the dining room.

I shake Mr. Monroe's hand and take a seat at the table next to Trevor, directly across from Ally. "Glad you can join us tonight, son," Mr. Monroe says.

"Thanks for inviting me," I say. It's the same exchange every time I accept one of their dinner invitations, but I don't mind. It's the only stability I've had in my life. I look across the table at Ally, and she makes a funny face at me, I try not to laugh out loud. These are the reasons I've come to love the Monroes. They're the most funny, kind, and down-to-earth people I've ever met.

***

"Pizza!"

"Pepperoni pizza!"

"No, it's a cookie!"

"Chocolate chip cookie?"

"Earth?"

"Seriously!" Alex yells. "Earth?"

"Alexander, you can't talk while you draw," Mrs. Monroe scolds.

"It's okay, mom. Time's up anyway," Ally says, trying not to laugh. She wasn't kidding, Alex is a horrible artist.

"What is it, son?" Mr. Monroe asks.

"Pimples," Alex says. "See," he says pointing to what I guess were supposed to be the eyes and the mouth of the face. "I started out with a smiley face, and then added the dots for the pimples."

"The mouth looks like a dot," Trevor says flatly.

"I'd like to see you do better," Alex challenges.

"I did do better, you guessed Jennifer Lopez right away."

"Because of the butt," Alex says. "It was a stick figure with a butt, not too hard to figure that out."

"Could have been Kim Kardashian," Ally supplies, causing me to laugh.

"What are you laughing at, big shot? You're up next," Alex taunts.

We've been playing Pictionary for about an hour now. I was teamed up with Ally and her mom, while Alex, Trevor, and their dad were on the other team. It turns out that I'm almost as bad at drawing as Alex is. "Almost" being the operative word. I can still draw a face that looks like a face.

I get up and pick a card from the deck. Are you serious? Of course I'd draw a card with an animal on it, and a chicken at that. This is going to be fun. Mr. Monroe flips the timer and I get started. My chicken must not look too bad, because Ally and her mom keep yelling out the names of various birds, so I know I'm on the right track. What else? Eggs! I draw a couple of ovals behind the chicken, and again I'm on the right track because they yell out 'eggs.' Finally, I draw a barn, and Mrs. Monroe calls out 'chicken.'

I look at Alex and grin. "Whatever," he rolls his eyes and everyone laughs.

We play two more rounds and our team wins. Ally jumps up and down, taunting Alex by claiming I was their secret weapon.

"Next week it's charades, bring your 'A game' Baker," Alex dares me.

"Please, I took two years of drama in high school, Monroe, you bring it," I challenge right back.

"Now, now, children," Mrs. Monroe chides, smiling because she knows we're just messing around. "Who wants dessert?"

Mr. and Mrs. Monroe are like the Cleavers. He's a very successful corporate attorney, which allows her to stay at home to raise the kids and keep house. They have dinner at home every evening, except for special occasions, and she's always baking something for dessert or a snack. Ally loves spending time in the kitchen, cooking and baking with her mom.

We all settle back at the table, which Mrs. Monroe had miraculously cleared at some point between dinner and our game. She set out a plate of brownies and goes around the table pouring milk. Like I said, the Cleavers.

"So, my little twinnies, what would you like to do for your birthday?" she sings out, using her term of endearment for Alex and Ally.

Alex looks over at Ally. "Don't you dare say it," he warns.

Ally looks at him innocently. "Whatever do you mean?"

"We're not going to Lombardi's," he tells her.

"Why not?" she asks. "It's the best restaurant around!" She looks genuinely appalled that he doesn't agree with her assessment. Lombardi's is a really great Italian restaurant that Ally chooses every time she's given the option.

"Why can't we do Taco Barn or Jose's?" Alex whines.

"Because you get the shits when you eat Mexican," Trevor laughs, earning a light smack on the back of his head from his mother for his language. "Sorry, Ma," he grins sheepishly.

"And besides," Alex continues, ignoring Trevor's comments, "you picked last year."

Ally sighs in resignation. "Fine. We will go where you want to go, but please no Mexican." She makes a face.

"How about Pizza Kingdom?" Alex asks.

"Isn't that for kids?" Mrs. Monroe asks.

Ally answers "yes" while Alex answers "no."

Mrs. Monroe looks to me and Trevor for the truth. "It's got arcade games and stuff," Trevor supplies.

"You can get pizza at Lombardi's," Ally tells Alex.

Alex rolls his eyes. "How about Joe's?" Joe's is a seafood restaurant and a pretty good one, too.

"I can agree to that," Ally says, surprising Alex with her quick consent.

"Sweet, I want some fried shrimp!" Alex pumps his fist in the air.

"Ok, so we'll go Saturday at six o'clock. Tell Joey," Mrs. Monroe says. Then she turns to me, "You're invited, too, Chase."

"Thanks, Mrs. Monroe. I'll be there." I haven't missed a Monroe birthday since I met Trevor in the fifth grade. I had just moved to Charlotte from a small town outside of Raleigh and he was my first friend, pretty much my only friend.

The twins were so much younger back then, first grade. At the time, you would never have guessed that more than ten years later we'd all hang out together and have anything in common. But Trevor always loved his little brother and sister, and as the twins grew up, Trevor kept them close. The four year age gap was irrelevant, and because they always hung out with Trevor, they were a lot more mature than other kids their age, even Alex.

We help Mrs. Monroe clean the kitchen and then I head home for the night. It's a school night for Ally and Alex, so there would be no hanging out in the garage until late. Mr. and Mrs. Monroe are pretty easy going most nights of the week, but they're firm that on Wednesdays and Sundays, the twins spend time studying or getting extra sleep.

I pull up in the parking lot of the small apartment my mom rents. I hate that I still live at home, especially at twenty-one, especially with her, but I'm saving my cash from the gigs we play to get a decent place. I don't want to move from one shit apartment to another.

When I get inside, I can see by the low light under my mother's bedroom door that she's in there, probably passed out with the TV on. Good, better to not have to deal with her drunk ass. Sadly, I'm not sure that I've ever really loved my mother. Not the way the Monroe kids love their mom, not the way *I* love their mom. But my mom was never that kind of mom, ever, at least that I remember. Maybe she was different before my dad left us when I was three. But I doubt it.

I sleep on a futon in the living room of the one bedroom apartment. The living room is basically my bedroom, containing all my stuff. I go to my dresser, which doubles as a TV stand, grab a pair of shorts and a t-shirt, and then head to the bathroom to change. When I return to my bed, aka futon, aka couch, I see a text notification from Ally.

**Ally:**  Thanks for helping beat Alex tonight!

**Me:**  no prob

**Ally:**  You already home?

**Me:**  yeah, just getting ready 4 bed.

**Ally:**  Already?

**Me:**  yeah, my mom is asleep so i figured i would take advantage of the quiet.

**Ally:**  Ok, well I won't keep you. Good night, Chase.

**Me:**      nite Al.


Ally knows about how my mom is from what I've told her and from what I'm sure Trevor has mentioned. So she knows peace and quiet around my house don't happen too often. I stretch and lay back on the futon, tugging the sheet over my body.

Like clockwork, the flashbacks begin almost immediately.


*There's a rhythmic banging coming from my mother's bedroom. I'm lying on my futon bed in the living room, with my pillows and blanket tight held against my head.*

*When I got home from Trevor's house, there was a party in full swing. I don't know why I didn't just accept Trevor's offer to sleep over, but we're twelve, almost teenagers, and teenage boys don't have sleepovers.*

*My mom has her "friends" over. And by friends I mean men–strange men. It's always the same. When I arrived, she moved the party to her bedroom, she has at least three of them in there now.*

*Now I hear her moaning and one of the men grunting. It's disgusting.*

*I'm not so young that I don't understand what's going on in there. My mother is a whore. I've known this for a few years now. She exchanges her body for drugs and alcohol.*

*I'm twelve years old–a kid and yet not. She took that from me, forcing me to live in this den of sin with her. It caused me to grow up faster than I should have. One too many times having to nurse her wounds when one of her men got out of hand or cleaning up her vomit will do that to a kid.*

*I pull the pillow tighter against my head, trying to drown out the sounds. The batteries in my CD player are dead, so I can't use my default escape–music. It'll be a while before I'm able to save up enough lunch money and spare change to buy new batteries, so the pillow and blanket will have to do.*

*Eventually the noises stop and I loosen my grip on the pillow. Hopefully it won't be long before the men are gone and I can rest easy. Having to be on alert sucks. At least it's the weekend. It's the worst when I have to stay alert on a school night. Sometimes they're still at it when I have to leave for school and I get no sleep.*

*I freeze when I hear the bedroom door open. Heavy footsteps make their way through the apartment, and I hear the familiar sound of the front door opening and closing. I exhale. Finally.*

*I remove the pillow from my head and roll over to face the room. My mother is sitting at the kitchen table in her flimsy robe, smoking a cigarette. Her normally pale face is flushed and she has dark circles under her eyes. She's only thirty-two, but she already has wrinkles by her eyes–they're not the happy laugh-line ones, either. They're the results of too much smoking, drinking, and drugs.*

*"I have fifty dollars here for you to get some groceries on your way home from school tomorrow," she says, not even looking at me. She must have heard the sheets rustle.*

*"Fifty bucks? Is that all you're worth?" I know I shouldn't disrespect my mother, but she's never done anything to earn my respect. Yeah, she didn't abort me, and she gives me a roof over my head and the occasional meal, but I've never felt loved or wanted, and that is more important.*

*"Don't sass me, boy," she spits out. She stubs out her cigarette and stomps off to her room. Moments later, I see the light go out. She didn't even shower.*

*I vow in that moment that I will never be like her. I will never be like the despicable men she has parading through here. I will never use sex the way that they do.*

I squeeze my eyes closed tight, willing the memories to go away. One day I will get out of this place. One day. That's the last thought I have before drifting off to sleep.

# Chapter Fifteen

As usual, we all spend most of our free time in the summer at the Monroes' pool. Ally is like a fish in the water. She participates in both the short- and the long-course seasons for a local swim club, so she's pretty much swimming all year round. When things went down with Blake and she was really upset, she stopped attending practice for a few weeks. Her mother eventually intervened and got her back on track. She has won many awards, so the coaches welcomed her back to the team. Now Ally's making up for it by swimming double the laps she usually does. I like seeing her focused and determined again, especially after that dark post-Blake period.

Tonight we're all attending one of Ally's swim meets. It's at an indoor community pool not too far from the Monroes' house. The place looks like a barn from the outside, complete with a red and white paint job, and inside it reeks of chlorine. There are giant ventilation fans humming near the ceiling to keep the air circulating, but I don't think it's working.

This is my first time attending one of these things, and my initial thought once I get inside, apart from the chlorine, is that the pool is massive. It looks to be about half the size of a football field and I am momentarily awe-struck by the fact that Ally swims that. I'm not in bad shape, I use my body a lot for work, but I think I'd pass out if I even attempted to do that.

Mr. and Mrs. Monroe lead us to our seats--bleachers alongside each wall, running parallel to the swim lanes. Trevor, Alex, Joey, and I settle in the back row, garnering some attention from surrounding females. Alex and Joey eat it up, while Trevor and I continue to take in our surroundings.

"I can't believe Ally swims in that," I say to Trevor.

"Wait 'til you see her, she moves so damn fast." He's completely cheesing, got the whole big brother thing going on right now.

"When is she up?" I ask, eager to see her in action. I've seen her swim in her pool, but that's small. She'll barely be a blip on the radar in this pool.

"The 400 meter is third," Trevor answers, looking at the program.

"400?" I ask, my eyes wide. "How many times is that?" I gesture back and forth down the lanes.

"Eight," he says nonchalantly.

*Eight?* Ally swims that eight times?

"And then the 800 is fifth."

"What?" I did the math, that's sixteen laps. "She's going to do twenty-four laps, total, in this pool?"

Trevor grins, "And she's going to win, too."

*Holy shit.*

About fifteen minutes later, a group of younger-looking kids take the platforms and do the 100 meter and 200 meter events. Ally is in the second heat for the 400 meter, which consists of the older age group, and it's next. Trevor is still studying the program, Joey and Alex are scoping out girls, and Mr. and Mrs. Monroe are speaking with other parents. I think I'm the only one currently bouncing in my seat, waiting for Ally to come out.

They call her group and everyone starts paying attention. Mrs. Monroe and Alex loudly cheer for Ally as they walk out. All the swimmers are dressed in identical black one-piece bathing suits and those cap things on their heads, so it takes me a moment to locate her. She's in the fifth lane and she is in the zone, staring straight ahead and practicing her breathing.

I'm trying not to check her out, to not think about her in that way, but it's difficult. She's in a bathing suit for crying out loud; and her curves that are normally covered by jeans and band t-shirts are right there for everyone to see. Yeah, I've seen her in a bathing suit before, but not when she's in her element like this. She's so confident, I'd be lying if I say it isn't attractive.

*Wait a minute...since when am I attracted to Ally? What the hell is that about?*

The announcer says some stuff I barely pay attention to–since I'm too busy wondering why the sight of my best friend's little sister is suddenly turning me on–and then the buzzer sounds and she's off. I'm instantly at the edge of my seat, watching her move under the water, one lap already down. She has amazing speed and she's at least a body-length ahead of the next competitor.

The six of us are standing and cheering as she completes her final turn. She's ahead by two body lengths now and she's absolutely going to win. It's exhilarating, and I'm not even the one racing. She taps the wall and our cheers are even louder than before.

Ally pulls her goggles off her head and looks up at the scoreboard, smiling broadly when she sees her time and position. She lifts herself out of the pool and receives hugs from her teammates and coaches. Finally, she turns to where we are standing on the bleachers, smiles and waves.

Her next event is much of the same. Ally annihilates the competition. It amazes me that she doesn't want to go pro with this, but she says she loves it too much to do it for a living. She doesn't want to lose the passion and says that training at the professional level is far too intense. I can sort of relate in my own way with the band. I love being a musician, but I wonder if my feelings would change if we did our thing professionally. I'll probably never get to find out, and that's fine because I love what we're doing now.

Once all the competitions are complete, we're finally able to meet Ally on the pool deck. She has changed into her team's track suit, and her long hair is hanging down her back, dry since she was wearing a swimming cap. I miss the bathing suit, but Ally is still beautiful. No, not beautiful. I do *not* think my best friend's little sister is beautiful. I don't think about her like that at all. *Right.*

She hugs her parents, then her brothers, then Joey, and then me.

"You were amazing," I say with a smile, squeezing her tight.

"Thank you," she blushes.

"Seriously, you kicked their as-butts," I quickly correct, chancing a glance at Mr. and Mrs. Monroe. Fortunately they're both talking to Ally's coach.

Ally laughs, it's a musical sound. *Musical? Where's my man card?*

"Thanks, I'm glad you came."

"I'm just sorry I missed the others. That was really entertaining."

She looks down and her blush deepens. That color looks good on her.

"You were awesome, as always," Alex says, suddenly appearing beside me.

"Thanks, guys."

"Hey, Al! Come on," one of her teammates calls out.

Ally looks over her shoulder and nods. "Just a minute." Turning back to us, she says "I'm going out with the team for dinner. I'll see you guys later?"

I can't say I'm not disappointed I won't get to spend more time with her this evening.

"Yeah," Alex answers. "We'll probably be in the garage."

"Okay," she smiles sweetly. She hugs everyone goodbye, saving me for last. "Bye, Chase," she whispers. When her soft breath feathers over my ear, goosebumps prickle across my skin. Yes, goosebumps. Don't judge.

"Bye, Al."

I watch as she walks away, and it's crazy, but I kind of feel like I miss her. I want to follow her. I want to go everywhere with that girl.

*What is going on?*

# Chapter Sixteen

Ally and Alex's senior year has finally begun. The twins are ecstatic that their high school years are finally coming to a close. Ally is her usual self, studying away and planning her future as a chef. She hopes to open her own sweet shop one day, and I can attest to the fact that she will succeed. The desserts she makes are delicious. Alex is his usual self, fooling around and getting by just enough for his parents to not give him grief about being in the band.

JACT was asked to join a local Battle of the Bands competition at the end of September. There's a big rock festival coming up in October, and the winner of the battle will get to open. Some bands we really like will be at the festival, so it would be a great experience for us, but we're all pretty nervous about the possibility of performing in front of such a large crowd. We're nervous about the competition, too. We've never done anything like it before, but apparently one of the radio station's DJs saw us play at the restaurant and liked what he heard. It gives us a little confidence, but not a lot.

The night of the battle, we are all nerves. We made it through to the semi-finals, but none of us know how. We were all off on our instruments at some point, and Alex even missed a lyric during our cover of a very popular song. Like I said, all nerves.

There are four bands in the semi-finals, us and three others. It's set up like a bracket, bands are pitted against each other until the very end, when there are two bands left and only one band can win. The other bands left are really good, and they haven't screwed up.

We're sitting in one of the back stage rooms of the club the competition is being held at, trying to psych ourselves up. There is another band back here with us, but not the one we'll be directly up against this round. They're staying to their side of the room and look completely chill. They probably do shit like this all the time.

The door to the room slowly opens and Ally's head appears in the gap. She sees us and her eyes brighten. "Hey!" She pushes the rest of the way into the room and I think I stop breathing.

Ally.

Sweet, innocent, Ally.

She's standing in front of us wearing a leather and lace corset-style top and black skinny jeans. She looks like a walking wet dream. Her friend Lucy is standing behind her, more conservatively dressed in jeans and a long-sleeve shirt. Lucy tends to focus on school more than anything else, so I'm sure she is feeling completely out of her element.

Trevor stomps over to Ally. "What the hell are you wearing?" he asks her in a hushed, angry tone.

"You don't like it?"

"You need to put more clothes on!" Trevor insists.

Ally rolls her eyes, "I'm not putting more clothes on. I think I look nice."

"I think you look nice, too!" one of the guys from the other band calls out from across the room. Ally blushes, but still thanks him because that's just how she is. Trevor shoots the guy a death glare. Joey and Alex are sitting on the sofa, watching the whole interaction with amusement. I don't think I've moved from my spot since she walked in the room. I did make sure my mouth was closed, though, and there was no drool.

"I just wanted to come back here and wish you all 'good luck.' You're doing awesome tonight, and I'm so proud of you."

Trevor visibly softens. "Thanks, sis."

Ally grins at him, assuming she's won this round. But I know Trevor, and he hasn't forgotten the sinful outfit his sister is wearing.

"But you're still not going back out there in that," he scolds.

"Trevor! I've been out there for the last few bands," Ally argues. She arrived late to the show because she had a swim meet she couldn't miss.

"And you're lucky I didn't see you then," he returns.

"But I don't have anything else to wear."

"Then I guess you'll have to stay back here."

Ally's mouth drops open and sadness fills her face. Oh, man. Why does she have to look so sad? I'm completely on board with Trevor here, I don't want her out there dressed like that for guys to drool over--I don't count--or even worse, to grope, but I don't want her to leave or have to hide out in the back either. Then I get an idea.

"Hold on," I tell them both and run to the corner of the room where there are boxes of Battle of the Bands t-shirts. I find a size small and bring it back over to her. "Here, put this on."

Ally takes the shirt, still looking disappointed, but looks up at me and gives a small smile. "Thanks, Chase."

My heart thumps in my chest. I love being the reason this girl smiles.

Ally pulls the shirt over her undergarments--because let's face it, that's what they are–and she seems to brighten up as she hangs out and talks with us. She talks about our competition and tells us why she thinks we're better than them, what we have that they don't, etc. She easily accomplishes what we were trying to do before she walked in, and now we're definitely psyched up and ready to get back on the stage.

\*\*\*

We lose in our semi-final round, but getting to be on stage and seeing Ally right up front cheering us on was worth the whole experience. We play better in our final set than we did any of the others, and I know it was because we have our biggest cheerleader there with us.

I text her later that night.

**Me:**      thx 4 coming 2nite.

**Ally:** Nowhere else I would have rather been. I'm just sorry I couldn't have been there earlier.

**Me:** dont b sry, its not like u ditched us, u had something important

**Ally:** I know, but I can't help but think I let you all down.

She thinks she let us down? Oh, hell no.

**Me:** stop it. u didnt let us down. we r all so proud of u 4 what you do in the pool. we wouldnt want u 2 miss that. U DID NOT LET US DOWN. got that?

**Ally:** Yeah, I got that. Thanks, Chase.

**Me:** ur welcome

**Ally:** I'm sorry you guys didn't win.

**Me:** its ok, we were a mess.

**Ally:** Did you have fun, though?

I think about it. Did I have fun? Heck yeah, I did. Playing music with my best friends, people cheering us on, making new fans...it was a blast.

**Me:**    yeah, i had a lot of fun.

**Ally:**    Then that's all that matters. I've lost my share of swim meets, but I still enjoyed being in the pool, doing my thing.


Ha. She's only lost a handful of times in the five years she's been swimming competitively. I know this because Mrs. Monroe was bragging about it at one of her meets this past summer.


**Me:**    liar

**Ally:**    What do you mean?

**Me:**    u never lose

**Ally:**    I do, too!

**Me:**    how many?

**Ally:**    It doesn't matter.

**Me:**    how many?

**Ally:**    Sigh. Four.

**Me:**    and how many have u won?

**Ally:**    Like 20 or something.

**Me:**    ...

**Ally:**    27

That is something else I already know, thanks to Ally's mom. Seventeen years old and she's won twenty-seven competitions. That's pretty significant considering she only competes once or twice every couple of months. She should be proud of that, not shy about it.


**Me:**     thats pretty cool Al

**Ally:**     Thanks. What you and the band does... that's pretty cool, too, Chase.

**Me:**     thx. nite Al

**Ally:**     Good night, Chase.

# Chapter Seventeen

Christmas at the Monroe house is an epic event. The day after Thanksgiving, the entire family goes to a nearby tree farm and actually cuts down a tree. They spend the rest of that day drinking eggnog or cider and singing Christmas carols--I'm not kidding. Then the guys do the outside lights and decorations, while the women take care of the indoor decorations. After dinner, everyone gathers in the living room and helps decorate the tree.

Like many other family events, Mr. and Mrs. Monroe have always invited me to join the family for their Christmas preparation festivities, but I have always declined. Until now. This year, I want to attend because spending extra time with Ally is like a gift, and I am not one to look a gift horse in the mouth.

Once all the intensive labor is through and we're all gathering in the living room to start on the tree, Trevor suggests I get my guitar so I can play along with the songs they are singing. I actually played the guitar in a Christmas concert at school one year, so I do know a few Christmas songs.

We go through the traditional songs, and then because we're JACT, we do a few rocking songs, too. Everyone is singing and Ally and her mom are dancing, occasionally grabbing one of the guys for a spin. And I'm jealous, because I'm stuck sitting on the couch with my guitar. But every once in a while, I catch her looking my way and wink, then smile at her instant blush.

\*\*\*

My mother and I are invited to my aunt's house, her sister, for Christmas Day. I don't want to go. I barely know this woman and it kind of pisses me off that she knows the way my mother is, yet hasn't ever tried to be more involved in my life. I see how the Monroes are with one another and that's the way a family should be.

In fact, Mrs. Monroe is the only reason I'm even going to my aunt's house. She told me that I didn't know the specifics about why my aunt hasn't been involved in my life and that I should give her a chance. If it turns out to be a positive thing, then I have more family. If it turns out to be negative, then I lose nothing. Mrs. Monroe tends to always be right.

Since I won't be around on Christmas, Mrs. Monroe insists I join the family on Christmas Eve. Joey is there, too, since he won't be around Christmas Day either. Of course, Mr. and Mrs. Monroe shower us both with gifts; it's all music-related so you can tell Trevor and Alex had a hand in it.

It's getting late and I'm running out of time. I got Ally a present, and it's not the CD, book, or movie type I can gift in front of everyone. And no, it's not lingerie either so get your mind out of the gutter. It's just kind of a big deal--not because it was expensive, but because of the thought I put into it.

Eventually I send her a text and let her know that I have a gift for my *friend*. She looks up at me after she reads it, immediately knowing that because I'm referring to our "secret friendship," the gift isn't something I can give her in front of everyone else.

She seems to consider our options, then texts me back that she'll meet me outside about twenty minutes after I leave. She says to be in "our spot," which I take to mean the side of the garage where I found her crying all those months ago. As much as I don't like the reminder, it's as good a place as any. I nod in her direction and start saying my thanks yous and goodbyes.

Once in place, I pull the little box out of my pocket. It's not wrapped because I can't wrap a present to save my life, but I did stick on a green and red bow. I just hope she likes it, and I hope it's not too much.

Almost exactly twenty minutes later, Ally comes outside. I notice she's got a small box in her hand as well. *She got me a present?* I smile at her and she smiles back.

"Hey," I say. Deep, right?

"I got something for you, too," she says, thrusting the box at my chest. Looks like she's about as nervous as I am to exchange these gifts.

"Thanks," I say, taking it from her hand. "This is for you," I hand her present over.

I look at my present and smile because it's not wrapped either; and like mine, it has a bow on top, only it's blue and silver. I want to see her reaction to her gift, so I wait to open mine until she's done.

She pops the lid on the box and her eyes widen. "Chase," she says softly. She fingers each of the charms on the bracelet: measuring spoons, a chef's hat, an apron, a cookbook, a whisk, and a mixer. There's room for more, and I figured I'd get her more in the future.

When she looks up to me, she has tears in her eyes. "This is perfect, thank you so much." She steps forward and wraps her arms around my neck. We've hugged before, but never like this. I can feel every inch of her body against mine, and it feels good. Then she pulls away.

"Open yours." Oh yeah, I have a present, too.

I open the box and inside is a silver guitar pick holder on a ball chain that can be worn like a necklace. Inside the holder are picks, and the one on top is sky blue and has a "C" etched in it.

"I love it. Thank you, Al." I fight to keep the emotion out of my voice. Like my gift to her, this was a heartfelt gift. Thoughtful. I rub my finger on the face of the personalized pick.

"It's the same color blue as your eyes," she says quietly, and I smile. A very thoughtful gift.

I lift the necklace over my head. I don't ever want to take it off. This girl completely disarms me and I have no idea what to do about it.

# Chapter Eighteen

After Christmas, things changed between Ally and me. It was like all of a sudden we went from talking about normal, everyday, friendly things like the band and Ally's plans for culinary school, to flirting. No, we aren't sexting or anything like that, but there's light teasing and, okay, maybe a few "what are you wearing" texts, but we're only joking when we say it. Isn't that how it always starts, though?

I'm finishing up at the construction site for my day job when a message comes through on my cell. I step out of the work zone and pull my phone out.

**Ally:** Are you busy?

**Me:** at wrk

**Ally:** I'm sorry

**Me:** whats up?

**Ally:** Just having a bad day, wanted to hear your voice.

Despite all the text-flirting, Ally and I haven't crossed the line to phone calls. So this is an unusual request. It's not a big deal, just a first for us. Especially during the day when I'm at work and she's at school. High school. Man, I'm fucked up.

**Me:** I take my brk in 20. call u then?

**Ally:** Thank you, Chase.

I should have just called her then since I'm completely useless for the next twenty minutes. I can't stop wondering what could have possibly happened to make her text me in the middle of the day like that. And she wants to hear my voice? That's different.

Finally I punch out for my break and walk off to find a quiet place away from the center of the job site. Scrolling through my contacts, I find her name and hit send.

"Hello?" her voice has an echo.

"Ally," I say. "Where are you? Why does it sound like you're in a cave?"

She giggles, I love that sound. "I'm sorry, I'm in the bathroom."

"Uh," I start, kind of disturbed that she's talking to me while in the bathroom. "Al, you're a cool chick and all, but I think that's crossing the line."

She giggles again, "I'm not going to the bathroom, silly. I'm just hiding out in here."

"Oh," well that's a relief. Sort of. Not sure I like that she's hiding out in the bathroom at school. "So what's going on?"

She sighs, "It's spring break for the colleges."

"Yeah?" I don't see why she would be upset about that.

"Yeah," she trails off and it all comes together.

"Blake?"

"Some girls in the locker room were talking about having seen him around town. I guess it kind of sounds stupid now that I'm saying it out loud. I don't know." She's starting to sound like that girl I found outside her house in the dark all those months ago.

"No, Ally. It's not stupid. He hurt you real bad, and he's been gone so you haven't really had to face it. You have a right to get upset that he's back." Not that I liked it very much. Not that I had a right to like it or not like it.

"I just worry that I might bump into him, you know? And last time I saw him, gosh. It was so embarrassing. I mean I caught him cheating, and *he* broke up with *me*, Chase. I *begged* him not to. I offered myself to him like a freakin' sacrifice."

She what? "You what?" Shocked doesn't even begin to describe what I'm feeling.

Ally is completely quiet on the other end.

"Al?" I ask.

"I'm here."

"What did you mean by that? Sacrifice?"

"It's nothing."

"It's not nothing."

"It's just when he broke up with me," she pauses.

"Al?"

"Sorry. When he broke up with me, I told him I'd do it with him if it would change his mind."

"What?!" I can't even believe she had offered herself to him like that! She was right, it *was* just like a sacrifice.

"I know, pretty pathetic, huh?" She sniffs. Dammit to hell. Now I've made her upset.

"I'm sorry, baby girl." Baby girl? What the hell is that about?

"Baby girl?" I could hear the small smile in her voice.

"Yeah," I smile back. "I don't know, it just seems to fit."

"I like it," she says quietly.

"Me, too," I say. And I do like it. But I also know this is trouble in the making.

"I feel a little better. I've got to get to my next class, though. Thanks for calling me, Chase. It means a lot."

"Anything for you, baby girl." We say our goodbyes and hang up.

I have no idea what this thing is between Ally and me, but it feels right. Even though I know I'll be mincemeat if Trevor and Alex ever got wind of it. Not to mention Mr. Monroe. The Monroes all love me, but that doesn't change the fact that I'm twenty-one and Ally is only seventeen. Not only is a relationship illegal, but it also borders on perverted. What the hell am I going to do?

Ally laid low the rest of that week. The band played a couple shows at a local hot spot since some of the college crowd were back in town for break, but our sets were over by ten, since Alex had school in the mornings. Ally didn't attend a single show, and for no reason apparently, since we never saw dipshit Blake.

***

A few weeks after the college spring break is the high school spring break. Since it's Alex and Ally's last high school spring break, Mr. and Mrs. Monroe rent their usual summer cabin at Lake Lure and invite everyone to join the family for the week. Joey and I join them, and Ally invites her friend Lucy, but she declines because her family is going on a trip as well. I can tell Ally is bummed, but since she'll be with us, I know she'll have a good time anyway.

We spend our days hiking the neighboring trails and boating on the lake. The water isn't warm enough to swim in, so our watersports are limited. We visit nearby Chimney Rock and hike to the top, taking pictures of all of us on what appears to be the top of the world. But most of our time is spent at the cabin hanging out, talking, playing games, and, of course, music. I can't remember the last time I had had so much fun.

We're leaving on Sunday, and Mr. and Mrs. Monroe surprise us all that Friday night, announcing that they're spending the night at a nearby resort that specializes in *Dirty*

*Dancing* nights. It's not the same resort that's in the movie, but apparently there's some obscure connection to the area, and *Dirty Dancing* is one of Mrs. Monroe's favorite flicks.

"You're gonna be gone all night?" Alex asks, completely surprised at the turn of events.

"Yes," Mrs. Monroe answers. "Trevor, Chase, and Joey are all adults. You and Ally are close enough. You're good kids and hang around alone at home enough. We trust you."

"Just behave yourself, Alexander." Mr. Monroe gives Alex a stern look, and I smirk. I know exactly what's going through Alex's head; he wishes he had met some chicks on this trip so he could party it up with them. I'm sure Trevor and Joey share similar thoughts.

"We'll be good, Mom," Ally assures her.

"I know you will, angel," Mrs. Monroe says back as she kisses Ally on the forehead.

"We will be back early tomorrow afternoon," Mr. Monroe says as he scoots his wife towards the door. "Make sure you clean up any mess you make."

"Have a good time," Trevor tells them as they walk out the door.

Their parents really don't have anything to worry about. We're good kids. Well, we're not exactly kids anymore, but you know what I mean. We don't drink excessively or do drugs, and we don't party with the rough crowds.

We end up hanging around the cabin watching reality TV, before finally watching a bad horror movie on demand. I'm cursing the movie choice until a scene startles Ally, who is sitting next to me on the couch, and she practically jumps into my lap.

Our eyes meet and she blushes, before breaking eye contact and scooting away from me. Before I can stop myself, I drop my arm that was resting on the back of the couch down to her shoulder and pull her back into my side.

Her eyes widen and she quickly looks around the room to see if anyone has noticed our new position, but they're all staring at their phones or the TV. She looks back at me, and I just shrug and go back to watching the movie. She eventually does the same.

When the movie is over, Ally bolts off the couch, out of my embrace, and brings the popcorn bowl into the kitchen. Joey suggests a fire in the pit on the back deck, and we all agree. We start the fire, and Ally comes out a few minutes later with all the makings for s'mores.

"You freakin' rock, little sis!" Alex says as he pulls her into a hug and spins her around.

"You're like four minutes older than me, Alex."

"That's still older," he grins.

"How is it you failed math freshman year? You're so smart." she taunts.

"Because that's the year you grew boobs, and people stopped thinking I was you and you were me."

"Alex, that doesn't even make sense," Joey adds.

"Yeah it does," Alex starts. "Before she had boobs, they'd think she was me so I'd get her good grades."

"That would only make sense if I ended up failing my tests," Ally says rolling her eyes. "And I never fail. Plus, we write our names on our papers, and we were never in the same classes." She pops him on the back of the head a minute later, making him drop his marshmallow into the fire. "And don't talk about my boobs!"

We all crack up at that. Alex and Ally bicker like cats and dogs, and most of the time it doesn't make any sense at all, but they're entertaining to watch. They're so similar in some respects, like their facial expressions and some of their mannerisms. But they're extremely different in the most overt ways, like their personalities. Alex is so outgoing he'll talk to anyone, while Ally is more reserved and saves her carefree attitude for those who are closest to her. Which basically means that when they're around us, they're more similar than not.

But they complement each other so well. It's like they're one complete person when they're together. When Ally was dating Blake, you could tell Alex missed her. He would zone out a lot and lose his focus. It was like something was missing from him. Since she has been hanging out again, he's been back to his usual self.

We made s'mores and tried to tell ghost stories, but we ended up getting in a marshmallow fight. Naturally, it stemmed from an Alex and Ally disagreement over the serial killer in Alex's campfire tale.

Just after midnight, everyone starts heading to bed. Ally is the first to go, followed by Joey and Alex, then Trevor.

"You want me to put this out?" Trevor asks, gesturing to the fire.

"Nah, man. I'll get it in a few." He nods and heads into the cabin, closing the sliding door behind him.

I lean back in my Adirondack chair and look up at the sky, at the moon in particular. I can just see it between a break in the clouds. It never ceases to amaze me that no matter where you are at night, it's always there. A constant.

"Whatcha doing out here all by yourself?" I jump at the sound of Ally's voice. I hadn't heard her open the door or walk up behind my chair.

She laughs. "Easy there, tiger. It's just me," she says as she walks around and takes a seat in the chair beside me.

"Sorry, didn't hear you come out." I turn to look at her face, but she's looking in the fire. She's even more beautiful in the glow of the firelight.

"Yeah, sure. You're just freaked out by Alex's super scary stories," she grins.

"You totally caught me," I laugh. "Thought you went to bed?"

She let out a puff of air, "I lied."

I raise my eyebrow in question, but she doesn't see it. She's still looking at the orange glow of the flames. "Everything okay?"

She finally looks at me and smiles, "It is now."

Now that she's here with me? I wonder.

"We haven't really had time to hang out together since we've been here," she tells me. "Or even talk really. I mean, it wouldn't exactly be inconspicuous if we sat there texting each other while in the same room."

"So you snuck out to hang out with me?" I ask obtusely.

She looks to me and smiles shyly, then nods. "I know it probably sounds weird and crazy, but I've missed you this week. You've been here the whole time, but I've missed you." She looks down and whispers the last part.

"It's not weird or crazy," I tell her.

"It's not?"

"No," I shake my head. "Because I've missed you, too."

She looks up at me in surprise, and her smile widens. "Really?"

"Yeah," I smile back.

"So you never did answer me," she says. I think back but I don't remember a question. She obviously sees the confusion on my face and adds, "What are you still doing out here?"

"Oh, nothing. Just looking at the moon." God, that sounds so stupid.

She looks up to the moon and nods. "Isn't it crazy how no matter where you are, it's always there? You can always see it."

My eyes shoot to hers, "That's exactly what I was thinking about."

"No way," she laughs.

"Yeah, seriously. I've always had an appreciation for the moon," I tell her.

Something about Ally makes me want to tell her everything.

"Why's that?" she asks.

"Growing up without my dad, and with my mom the way that she was, I never really had anything constant in my life. The moon was my constant. When my mom would have one of her parties, I'd always sneak out to the fire escape of the apartment and stare up at the moon. It would always be there, you know? My dad wasn't there. My mom was there, but she wasn't there for me. So I guess I latched onto the one thing I knew would always be there."

I'm not sure why I shared all that with her. She's quiet now and when I look over at her, it looks like she has tears in her eyes. "What is it, baby girl?"

She smiles at the name, "I'm just so sad for you, Chase. What you must have gone through. I can't even imagine. It just makes me appreciate my parents that much more. I'm sorry if that sounds callous."

"It's not callous. I feel the same way. I mean how I appreciate your parents. I don't know how much they know about my mom, but they know enough to treat me like one of their own kids without me having to say anything. They're awesome people."

"They are," she agrees.

I lean back in my chair, looking up to the sky again.

"This is nice," Ally says after a minute.

"What is?" I ask, thinking that this entire evening, hell, this entire week, has been a lot more than nice.

"This," she says, using her hand to gesture between us. "Talking and all. I mean, we text all the time and now we're sitting here and we can say whatever we want. So, what's next?" she laughs, turning to me with a playful look. "The weather?"

"It *was* a nice day today," I say with a straight face and she laughs. "So what *do* you want to talk about?" I ask her.

"I don't know. *Not* the weather."

"Your senior year is almost over," I offer.

She sighs, "Yeah."

"Are you not happy about that?"

"No, I am," she says.

"Then what is it?"

"When we talk about school, it just reminds me of our age difference is all."

That is a problem. Isn't it? *Yes, Chase, you're four years older than her.* The age difference is an issue.

"Nothing could ever happen," she says quietly, sadly.

Part of me is jumping up and down at the fact that she would want something to happen between us. But the other part of me is just as upset as she is that we will never be able to explore whatever this is between us.

"It's for the best," I say, and I'm not sure if I'm trying to convince myself or her.

"It's just bullshit, though, isn't it?" She stands up and begins to pace. "If we were ten years older, four years wouldn't be an issue. It's because I'm seventeen. It's because I'm not even legal yet that it's a problem."

Actually, the legal age of consent in North Carolina is sixteen, but I'm not about to let her know that I know that. Or why I know that. No, I was not doing Internet research to see if I would get put in jail for flirting with her over texts. Not. At. All.

She went on. "It shouldn't matter. Age shouldn't matter. I mean, it doesn't matter, does it? We all hang out all the time, and we're all equals. No one pays attention to our age difference when we hang out together as a group."

I stand up and block her path. Putting my hands on her shoulder, I say, "Ally, take a breath."

"I really like you, Chase." And I swear my heart skips a beat.

"I really like you, too, Ally." She licks her lips, and my eyes dart down to them.

"It's not fair," she sniffs.

I look back up to her eyes, and they're filled with tears. "Oh, baby girl, don't cry." I pull her into my chest and wrap my arms around her, resting my chin on her head.

"Chase, I know there are consequences..." she trails off.

"We'll figure it out, Al," I tell her. I don't even know what I'm trying to say, I'm just hoping to calm her down.

She pulls away from me and looks up with her tearstained face. Her beautiful, tearstained face. "What will we figure out?" she asks.

"I don't know," I say honestly, shaking my head. "I don't know."

"But you feel it, too?"

I sigh, then I nod. "Yeah, baby girl. I feel it, too."

The corner of her mouth raises just a little, and she rests her head back against my chest. "I didn't mean for it to happen," she says.

"Me neither."

"What are we going to do? I can't ignore what I feel for you, Chase," she says, desperately. "I can't."

"Okay, calm down, baby girl. We will figure something out." I run my hand up and down her back in a soothing gesture.

"I'm sorry," she whispers.

"Don't be. I can't seem to resist you either."

"Yeah?"

"Yeah, baby girl."

She pulls back and looks up at me. She licks her lips again and looks at mine. Oh God, why is she looking at me like that? Why does she have to lick her lips? And why is she looking at mine? I'm trying to be a good guy here, but I'm still only human.

"Ally?"

"Chase?"

"What are you doing?"

"I'm trying to figure it out," she says just before she lifts up on her toes and presses her lips against mine.

And I. Am. Gone.

I grab on to her shoulders and pull her body closer to mine. She opens her mouth in a gasp, and I take it as an invitation. Our tongues dance with one another, and I can't get enough. Neither can she. Her arms are around my neck now, pulling me down closer. I can't get any closer. She can't get any closer. If we could crawl inside each other at this moment, we would. I guarantee it.

A sudden crack of thunder finally breaks us apart. We're standing, panting, about a foot from each other. Soaking wet.

When did it start raining?

Ally looks around at the wet deck and the smoke lifting from the extinguished fire. Then she looks back at me, smiles, and laughs. Like a full on body laugh.

"Not doing much for my ego here, Al," I say, only slightly joking.

She straightens up and steps closer to me, removing the distance between us. Taking my face in her hands and looking into my eyes, she tells me, "Your ego has nothing to worry about, Chase Baker." Then she kisses me. Again. And it's amazing. Again.

By the time we finally go inside, we're soaked to the bone. Ally can't stop giggling, obviously just as high as I am about what happened between us outside. She's holding my hand as we move through the cabin as quietly as we can. It's not working because our wet feet are making squish noises with each step, further encouraging the giggling.

I walk her to her bedroom door and give her a quick kiss goodnight before making my way to the second floor where the rest of the guys and I are staying. I strip to my boxers in the bathroom and dry off as much as I can before sneaking into the room I'm sharing with Trevor. Thank God, he's still asleep. I don't want to do any explaining tonight.

I lay in bed and listen to the rain. Tonight Ally and I crossed a line. A line we probably—no, definitely—shouldn't have crossed. A line that could destroy everything we know. But there's no way in hell I'm going back over to the other side.

# Chapter Nineteen

"Shh," I whisper, and she giggles again. "Ally," I say, firmly this time.

"That tickled," she laughs. We had family dinner tonight, and I hid out in the backyard after driving my car around the corner, waiting for Ally to slip out. Evidently, it tickled when I grabbed her as she rounded the side of the house.

"Not was I was going for, baby girl." A heated look comes across her face, and she pushes me against the side of the house and plants her lips on mine. Her arms wrap around my neck, and my hands go to her waist. When she pulls me in tighter her shirt slips up and I feel skin. I groan. "Baby girl, we gotta stop."

She shakes her head, telling me no, but I pull away. "Chase," she whines.

"Ally, you really test my control. You know that, right?"

She smirks and lifts up onto her toes to kiss me again. I give in, because she tastes so damn good; it's too hard to resist, and I pull her body into mine. She moans in approval, and it takes all I have, literally, all I have, to pull myself away from her.

She has the most adorable pout face. Too bad she overuses it.

"Sorry, baby girl. You need to go back inside, it's a school night."

She rolls her eyes. It's her typical response when I mention school. "Whatever."

I kiss her on the tip of her cute nose and hug her close. "I'll miss ya until I see ya."

"Me too," she whispers. I pat her on the ass as she walks away, and I certainly don't miss the glare she shoots me before she rounds the corner.

I lean back against the house and wait a few minutes before heading around to the front of the house. Just as I break from the tall hedges that line the house, I bump straight into Alex.

"Shit! You scared the hell out of me."

"What are you doing back here?" he asks, tilting his head to the side.

"Thought I heard something," I lie.

"Didn't you go home?"

"Forgot my keys."

"Was Ally just back here?"

"I didn't see her." The lies come out too easily. I feel like such a jerk.

"I just saw her come from this way," he presses.

"Maybe that's what I heard then?" I offer. I think I'm playing it cool on the outside, but internally I'm freaking out. "But I didn't see anyone when I got back there."

He looks at me questioningly for another moment, then nods. "Yeah, okay." Sadly, he has no reason to think I'd lie to him. I'm the worst kind of friend.

We both turn and walk to the front of the house. "See you tomorrow?"

"Yeah, see ya, Chase."

That was close. Too close.

\*\*\*

It's a Friday night and I'm in the garage with the guys, practicing a new song to play at our gig the following night.

"Where's Ally?" Trevor asks. She's been a staple around the garage during practices again, so it's unusual for her to be missing.

"Out with Lucy," I answer.

"How do you know?" Alex asks, and I still. *Shit*. I know because she texted me. I know because I know everything she does, just like she knows everything I do. I know because I can't keep my mind off of her for a minute. But I can't tell her brother that. I can't tell my best friends that.

"Heard her mention it yesterday," I quickly cover.

He nods in acceptance, and I feel like a total asshat. Like Alex, my best friend has no reason to think I'm lying to him. I never have before. We're as close as brothers, as close as he and Alex are. As close as he and Ally are, maybe even closer since she's a chick and all.

"Yeah, they're going dress shopping or some shit. They were talking about it at lunch." Alex adds, giving me an odd look. To be honest, I'm a little nervous around him after he almost caught me and Ally the other night.

"Dress shopping?" Why don't I shut my big fat mouth? But I can't help it, she didn't tell me she was dress shopping.

"Yeah, for graduation," Alex says.

"That's still two months from now," I say.

"How the hell would I know? Girls do weird shit." Alex says. "I'm going commando under my gown."

And he says girls do weird shit. Joey laughs while Trevor and I shake our heads. "That's a visual I didn't need, bro," Trevor says.

"Let's take it from the top, boys," Joey says, starting us off with the beat for the first song on our set list.

We have about a dozen original songs, and the rest we do are covers of bands like Three Days Grace, Theory of a Deadman, and some of the softer Stonesour hits. Our set list consists of about half and half. We've tossed around the idea of cutting our own demo to sell at our shows and send off to labels, but we decided to wait until after Alex graduates so we have the time to dedicate to it without pulling his attention from school any more than being in the band already does. Mr. and Mrs. Monroe have been supportive of the band, and we don't want that to change.

We play through the set list one last time, and I rush out of there, eager to get home and talk to Ally.

***

"I almost slipped up today," I tell Ally when we're talking on the phone later that night.

"How?" she asks nervously.

"At practice, Trev asked where you were and I told him you were shopping. Alex asked how I knew, and I freaked. I told them I overheard you mentioning it yesterday."

She laughs. Laughs. I gave myself a minor heart attack earlier, and she thinks it's funny. It's the same reaction I got when I told her about my run-in with Alex the other night. Apparently she had gotten the same line of questioning from him, and fortunately, somehow, our stories matched up.

"Not funny, baby girl."

"It's kind of funny."

"Wouldn't have been funny if he beat my ass."

She sighs, "We're going to have to tell them eventually."

"But I like my face," I whine.

"I like your face, too, baby. But you know the longer we wait, the worse it will be." She's got a point, but that still doesn't mean it's going to be good when we tell them.

"I know, baby girl. I just wish we could stay in our little bubble forever."

"I don't," she says sassily. "I want to shout from the roof tops that you're my man."

I laugh. "And I want to shout that you're my girl."

"Swoon."

"Did you just say 'swoon'?" I laugh.

"Shut it, Baker."

I laugh harder. "You're such a girl sometimes," I joke because we always tease her at practice when she acts like a girl because she's always been one of the guys. She's not 'one of the guys' to me anymore, but I still have to pretend.

"Yeah, but you like me as a girl," she flirts.

Ain't that the truth? "That I do."

"And I like you as a boy."

"Man."

"Same parts," she says flippantly.

"Bigger parts," I return.

"Can test that theory?"

I groan. She's killing me. "Yes." I hear her gasp. "Which is exactly why you shouldn't."

I hear her huff. "One day, Chase Baker. One day."

I don't know if that's a threat or a promise, but it feels like both.

***

It's rare that Ally and I are ever alone together when we're not hiding behind a corner or in the dark. Sneaking around isn't fun, especially when you each spend about seventy-five percent of your free time with the people you're trying to sneak around on.

But Mr. and Mrs. Monroe took Trevor and Alex to Guitar Center to get some accessories they needed. Usually Trevor and Alex would go alone, since both are clearly old enough to drive and shop without their parents, but I think Mr. and Mrs. Monroe tagged along because they want Alex to point out the guitar he's had his eye on, so they can get it for him as a graduation or birthday present. I play guitar in the band, and Alex sings, but he's always been interested in learning the guitar and, personally, I think it would be cool to have a second guitar in the band. Alex insists he doesn't want to play on stage, but we will see what happens.

So Ally and I are alone. In her room. No brothers. No parents. Just us.

*Just us.*

And Ally is wearing skimpy little boy shorts with a skimpy little tank top.

Fuck my life.

"Ally," I groan. "Will you put some pants on or something?"

"It's hot," she says as she shrugs one shoulder.

"It's hot," I mimic in a high pitched voice that doesn't sound anything like her.

She laughs as she fiddles around with her iPod. She finally finds what she's looking for and pops the gadget in the docking station, allowing music to pour through the speakers.

"What's this?" I ask. She usually listens to hard rock, and this isn't hard rock. It has a sexy, bluesy sound.

"Mazzy Star," she says. "'Fade into You' is the name of the song. I heard it in *Starship Troopers,* and loved it." She's walking towards me slowly, swaying her hips back and forth. She stops about two feet in front of where I'm sitting on her bed and motions for me to come to her with her finger.

Because I absolutely can't resist her, I stand up and take the one step necessary to be standing right in front of her. She wraps her arms around my shoulders and rests her head on my chest. "What are you doing?" I ask.

She removes her arms from my shoulders, grabs my hands, and places them on her waist. Then she puts her arms back on my shoulders and rests her head on my chest again. "We're dancing, ya big goof."

I smile and wrap my arms all the way around her waist to pull her closer to me, resting my cheek on top of her head. We move back and forth at the foot of her bed for the length of the song and a few other similar ones that follow it.

"I like this," I admit.

"Me too," she says.

"Everything okay, baby girl?" I ask.

"Everything is perfect," she tells me.

I want to tell her I love her because I do. In this moment, I'm certain that I'm in love with this beautiful girl I'm dancing with. But I don't tell her. I can't tell her. This is all so crazy. A whirlwind even. A year ago we were just blips on one another's radar, and now? I don't think I could live without her.

And everything about that is wrong.

Her family would kill me. They would think I'm taking advantage of her, simply because I'm so much older than she is. I know I'm not taking advantage, she wants this as much as I do. But I'm supposed to be older and more responsible. Her parents trust me for Christ's sake. Her brothers are my best friends, my brothers.

And the age difference. She wasn't wrong when she said that ten years from now it wouldn't matter. If she was twenty-seven and I was thirty-one, no one would care. But seventeen is the key word here. She can't even vote yet, buy cigarettes, or play the lottery. Our relationship might not be illegal, but she's not even considered an adult yet, and I've been able to vote for three years.

"Whatcha thinking about?"

I hadn't realized I'd stopped moving. She's looking up at me with those gorgeous baby blues, and I sigh. "Nothing, baby girl."

"Don't lie to me, Chase," she takes a step back until she's out of my arms.

"What are we doing here, Ally?"

She cocks her head to the side. "What do you mean?"

"This," I say, gesturing between us. "What is this? What do you want it to be?"

Her eyebrows pinch together as she tries to figure me out. "What do you want it to be?"

I sigh in frustration and run my hands through my short hair. "Don't do that, Al. Don't answer my question with a question. I'm being serious here."

"I see that," she snaps.

I groan, "Don't get mad now."

"I'm sorry if I'm too emotional for you," she huffs. "I thought we were on the same page."

"We are on the same page."

"Then why are you asking me this? What's going on in your head?"

"I don't know," I practically growl out, causing her to take a step back. "I'm sorry, baby girl. I'm just freaking out a little bit. This is going to affect our entire lives. You do realize that, don't you?"

"Of course I realize that!"

Jeez, I'm fucking this all up. She has never yelled at me before.

"What? You think because I'm still a teenager that I'm just a stupid kid? That I don't understand the consequences of my actions? Well I understand them just fine, Chase. I know that my being with you can turn my family against me, against you, and I can't care. I just can't care because I can't picture my life without you in it right now. I don't care if I have to hide in a damn closet for the rest of my life. As long as you're in that closet with me."

Her cheeks are wet with tears and her eyes are the saddest I've ever seen them. I did this. I take a step towards her, but she takes another step back. I frown, "I'm sorry, baby girl. I'm so sorry. I wasn't questioning what we have."

"You were," she interrupted, crossing her arms in front of her in a defensive gesture.

"I wasn't. I just worry about the future is all. I don't want your family to be upset with you. They're your life. I know you'd be devastated if they were upset with you."

"They're my family. They may be upset about us being together, but they wouldn't disown me. I think you're more worried about you."

What? This isn't the direction I wanted this conversation to go in. I just wanted to make sure she knows that it isn't just us who will be effected by our relationship. Whether they end up unhappy about the arrangement or not, they'd be hurt by us hiding it more than anything. Our dishonesty.

"Ally, baby girl, I'm not worried about me. I'm worried about—"

"Bullshit!" she yelled.

"Damn it, Ally!" I rake my hands through my hair again. "Shut up for a minute!" She glares at me; I've never seen her like this before. So angry. She wasn't even this angry over Blake. I take a cautious step towards her, and again, she takes a step back. I curse under my breath. "Baby girl, why are you running from me?"

"Because you don't feel for me the way I feel for you," she cries, and she collapses down onto her bed behind her, folding in on herself. The sight completely breaks my heart.

I sit down beside her and pull her into my lap, despite her struggles and sobs. I kiss her hair and run my hand up her back. "It's okay, baby girl. I'm here and I'm not going anywhere."

"You're gonna leave me," her voice is scratchy from the sobs.

"I will never leave you," I promise.

"Yeah, you will," she sobs harder.

I try to lift her chin, and she fights me. Using both hands, I pull her face up to mine. "I will never, ever leave you." I can see in her eyes the moment she believes me, and I exhale in relief, pulling her tight into me. "God, baby girl. Don't ever doubt the way I feel about you. You damn near tore my heart out just now. I don't want to see you like that. So upset? It killed me."

"I thought you were trying to find a way to stop seeing me," she hiccupped.

"No, I don't want to stop seeing you. Not at all. I'm just worried about hurting your family is all. I know they mean the world to you, and they mean the world to me, too. I know that hiding this is going to hurt them, and that makes me upset."

"It makes me upset, too, Chase. But what else can we do? No one would understand."

"I know. I don't know what else we can do. But I do know that I don't want to let you go."

"I don't want to let you go either. I... I think I'm falling in love with you," she whispers the last part.

I lift her chin and kiss her lips. "I'm already so in love with you."

She smiles and kisses me again. After a few minutes, I pull away and immediately laugh.

"What's so funny, Baker?" she asks with her hands on her hips.

"You look like one hot mess," I tell her.

She stands and walks over to the round mirror above her dresser and gasps. Her hair is sticking up in all different directions and her make-up has run all over her face. She screeches and slaps my arms as she runs past me and out her bedroom door, presumably to the bathroom to wash up.

I lay back on her bed and sigh. That was a close call. But I know she's only that emotional because all this sneaking around is taking as much of a toll on her as it is me. She's so close with her family, her parents and her brothers. It has to be killing her to not be able to share this with her mom. They're practically like sisters, they're so close. We need to come up with a plan.

I try to think of ways of how we can we tell her family, but before I get too deep into thought, Ally returns to her bedroom, struts right up to me, and sits, facing me, straddling my lap.

"We just had our first fight, Chase. Do you know what that means?"

I can't speak with her sitting on me, so I shake my head back and forth.

She giggles and wriggles her eyebrows, "It means it's time to make up." She leans forward, wraps her arms around my neck and fuses her mouth against mine.

What was it I wanted to do? I can't think about much of anything anymore.

# Chapter Twenty

Things are heating up even more between Ally and me. We still haven't done more than make out, much to her disappointment. The age difference and secrecy clearly bother me more than her, not that she's completely unperturbed about it. Anytime I say anything that alludes to it, she gets distant. It's like she wants to stay in our own little bubble when we're together and forget the outside world exists. It's all well and good in theory, but not so much in practice.

It's a Saturday night and we managed to arrange some alone time. The band doesn't have a gig because the restaurant we normally play at is closed for renovations this week. Ally managed to convince Alex to ask out a girl he's been eyeing at school, Joey picked up a shift at work, and Trevor is hanging out at home. I told him I had a date, which wasn't a lie, and Ally said she was going out with Lucy.

I'm taking her out to Mountain Island Lake. I packed a picnic-style dinner, complete with a red and white checkered blanket. We lay on the blanket, feeding each other cheese cubes and grapes, talking and laughing.

It never gets old. Every single day is a brand new day with Ally and times like these, when we get to share real dates, it's even more amazing. I know how cheesy that sounds, but it's true. We could share the same story over and over again, we've done it, and it's like hearing it for the first time.

She's talking about graduation, which is only a month away now, and she's so animated about it. She has the biggest smile on her face, and she's moving her hands around as she talks. It's fascinating, and I can't get enough.

"Stop staring at me like that, you creeper!" she laughs, throwing a grape at me. It bounces off my nose and falls to the blanket between us.

"Hey now, don't you waste the fruits of my labor," I tease. I pick up the grape and pop it in my mouth, grinning at her. "And I thought you like it when I look at you."

"I do, but it was like you were participating in a one-sided staring contest."

"It's because you're so beautiful I can't get enough of you," I tell her.

She sighs dreamily and her eyes cloud over. 'Swoon,' I believe is the term. "You're such a romantic." She leans forward and gives me a quick peck on the lips, but I surprise her by pulling her down onto me and deepening the kiss. I hold back my groan as she moans in response. She pulls back just enough to look in my eyes and say, "I can't get enough of you either."

We alternate between making out, snacking on the remaining fruit I brought for dessert, and talking while looking up at the stars and the moon.

"Every time I look at the moon, I think of you," she says.

I roll my head to look at her lying beside me. "I think of you, too."

She rolls her head over to look at me and smiles. Just as I'm leaning in to kiss her, her phone rings. She grumbles something under her breath about 'timing' and I laugh. She sits up and digs in her bag for her phone.

"It's Lucy, I better answer it since I used her as my cover tonight. I hope my parents didn't call over there looking for me because I'd be in so much trouble." She makes a face, then slides her finger across the phone to answer the call. "Hey, Luce, what's up?"

I'm not listening to what she's saying, just watching her mouth move as she speaks. I can't even stop myself from sitting up and kissing her.

She pulls away from me and swats at me. "Sorry, Luce. What were you saying? Nothing, just hanging out. I'm not doing anything. What noise? I don't know what you heard, but I'm just watching some TV." She's glaring at me the whole time and I can't help but laugh quietly. "No, I'm alone. Look, the movie is getting to a good part, and I can't find my remote to pause it. I'll call you later? Okay, tomorrow. Yeah, bye."

She taps the screen to cut off the call and puts her phone back in her bag. "You think you're so cute, don't you?" she scolds as she lays back down and then rolls on top of me.

I smile at her, "You've got a purdy mouth."

She busts out laughing at my *Deliverance* impersonation, though it was geared more towards Woody Harrelson in *Zombieland*, one of our favorite movies. I start laughing, too, and pretty soon we're kissing again.

"Will it always be like this?" she asks after a while.

"Absolutely."

"Promise me?"

I look over at her, the moonlight making her blue eyes shine. "I promise, baby girl. As long as we've got our moon, we'll have each other. I love you."

Her eyes fill with emotion, "I love you, too, Chase Baker. Forever."

"Forever," I agree and then she laughs. "Care to share what's so funny about that?"

She looks at my serious expression and laughs harder. "I'm sorry," she squeaks out. "I'm not laughing at that. It's just, oh my God, this is embarrassing."

"Did you fart?"

She sits up and her eyes widen as her mouth forms an 'O.' "Chase!"

"What? Everybody does it," I say, completely straight-faced.

"I can't even believe you right now. That is *not* why I was laughing."

"Well, you said it was embarrassing."

She sighs, "That would be mortifying. Embarrassed isn't even the right word."

"They're synonymous."

"Thanks for the English lesson."

"Sorry, what were you gonna say?" She actually looks a little shy now. I sit up and pull her into my arms. "What is it, baby girl? You know you can tell me anything. Forever, remember?"

"It's lame," she says quietly.

"Nothing you say is ever lame."

"That was lame," she laughs.

"Tell me," I insist.

"If this is really forever, then one day I might be a baker named 'Baker.' Told you it was lame," she says so quickly I can barely make out the words.

I'm stunned silent. Ally having my last name? Allyson Baker. Allyson Marie Baker. Mrs. Chase Baker. Now who is the lame one?

"Say something?" she asks nervously.

"Allyson Baker," I say. "I like the sound of that."

"Really?" she looks up at me.

"Hell, yeah," I nod. "Someday, Ally. Someday you will have my name, and I'll give you everything you could ever dream of."

She smiles at me. "Just give me you. *You're* everything I've ever dreamed of."

"I promise," I say as I lean in to give her a quick kiss. Then I jump to my feet and reach out my hand for her to take.

"What are you doing?" she asks, giggling.

I pull my phone out of my pants pocket and scroll through the songs until I come to the playlist I made for tonight. I press play and put it in my shirt pocket so we can still hear it, then I pull her in close. I mirror our positions from that night in her bedroom and she quickly catches on.

"I love this song," she says as "Easy to Love You" by Theory of a Deadman starts playing.

I start singing the words to her, about moonlight and wishing she will never leave because she's all that I'll ever need. When I look into her eyes, they're full of tears. I frown.

"They're happy tears, baby." She rests her head back on my chest, and I continue singing to her.

Yeah, I made a playlist of love songs just for our date tonight. I'm not ashamed. I hold Ally in my arms, and we dance through all ten songs, right there under our moon and its stars.

***

It's a few days before Ally's graduation and I have finally come up with a plan. I'm meeting her outside of her house tonight after practice to share it with her. She'll either love it, or it'll totally freak her out. It really could go either way and with Ally, you just never know. She's always surprising me.

Like the other day when I gave her an early graduation/birthday gift, a necklace with matching earrings. The gemstone was alexandrite, the less common birthstone for June. She whisper-yelled at me for spending so much money when I was trying to save up to get out of my mother's apartment. Then, because she loved the jewelry so much, we made out for an hour in the dark in her backyard. In that case, she loved it *and* she totally freaked out.

I was about to find out what response I was going to get since we just wrapped up our last song and started putting our instruments up.

"Just a few more days left," I say to Alex, referring to his graduation on Saturday.

"Thank God. It's ridiculous that they even require attendance this week."

"Can't you just skip that shit?" Joey asks.

"No. If any seniors miss a day this week they don't walk on Saturday."

"Can they do that?" I ask. I don't remember that rule from when I graduated. Shit, I was probably the reason they came up with that rule with the way my attendance record was as a senior.

"Yeah. We'd still get our diploma and all, but we wouldn't be able to participate in the ceremony."

"And mom would freak the fuck out if that happened," Trevor adds, and Alex nods.

"Crazy," Joey says, shaking his head. I think some days he regrets dropping out, but other days he loves the freedom too much. Plus, I know he needs the money from his day job, and he couldn't get that while going to school, too.

"Yeah, but just three more days, and it's all over. I can't wait. No more 'Alex, time to wake up,' or 'Alex, it's a school night.' Or my favorite, 'Alex, don't forget to do your homework.'" The guys and I laugh at his damn near perfect impersonation of his mother.

"Okay, well, I will see you guys tomorrow for dinner," I say as I pass out fist bumps. "See you Thursday, Joe."

"Later, man."

I leave the garage and head down the driveway to my car. I shouldn't have been so eager to get out of there, because I still have to wait for them to leave before I sneak back up. I start my car and fiddle around with the radio for a little bit, waiting to see them to exit the garage so I can pull off and know it'll be safe to come back. On nights when I'm meeting Ally, I drive around the corner after Joey leaves and walk back.

Thankfully I only have to wait about a minute before they exit. I roll down my window and do the usual, offer Joey a ride home. He never drives, always walks, since he lives just around the corner. And as usual, he declines. I wave and drive off, circling the block to give Joey time to get home before parking around the corner.

The anticipation gets the best of me, and I practically run back to the house. When I get around back, Ally is waiting for me.

"Hey there, good looking," she smiles.

"Hey, baby girl." I step up to give her a quick kiss, but she grabs hold of my shoulders and pulls me in closer. I groan and pull back. "I gotta talk to you."

Her brows pinch, and she frowns. "Is something wrong?"

"No, baby girl. Nothing is wrong at all," I assure her, pulling her back into my chest for a hug. "I have a plan."

"A plan for what?" I pull back and brush her hair back behind her ears, which results in a glare. She hates it when her hair is behind her ears. She shakes her head out like a dog and I laugh.

"A plan to tell everyone about us," I say on a big exhale.

She sighs. "Yeah? And what's that?" I can tell she's a little bit frustrated, I know she doesn't like talking about this. But that's too bad. I'm not going to continue to sneak around like I'm ashamed of our relationship. I love her and I want the world to know it.

"Let's tell them on Sunday."

"This Sunday?"

"Yes."

"That's your grand plan?" She looks at me in disbelief. "To tell them on my birthday? What, do you think they'll be less upset with me on my birthday?"

Now it's my turn to sigh. "No, you silly girl. Well, it's part of it. But it's not to cushion the blow."

She raises an eyebrow at me. "Then, why then?"

"Well, you'll be eighteen on Sunday."

"I know, we've talked about the benefits of me turning eighteen," she grins and wriggles her eyebrows. We decided to wait to do anything more than kissing until after she turns eighteen. And I mean *anything* other than kissing. We haven't touched, groped, or fondled, and we've barely even caressed. And she just loves reminding me about it.

I roll my eyes. "You have a one-track mind, baby girl."

"You love my mind," she smarts.

"I love everything about you," I return, and she melts into me.

"How did I get so lucky?" she asks.

I know it's rhetorical, but I answer anyway. "The same way I did."

"So what else does this plan of yours entail?" she asks, getting back on point.

"Well, we tell them on Sunday because you're eighteen. So not only does it look better that you're eighteen and I'm still twenty-one, but you'll also legally be an adult."

"And? They'll still kick our butts if they want to."

"True," I agree. Here goes nothing. "But if things go south, you'll be old enough to come live with me."

She lets out a short gasp and looks up at me, caution in her eyes. "Live with you?"

"Yeah. I have enough money saved to get my own place. And if things don't go well with us telling your family, you can always come stay with me until things cool down. We could get a place near your school."

"You want me to live with you?" she asks. That's obviously the only thing she heard.

"Yeah," I nod. "If you want to."

"I want to," she says immediately, surprising me. I think it surprised her, too, because her eyes widened as soon as she said it. "I mean, if you really want me to."

I laugh, "I wouldn't have said it if I didn't mean it. But I don't want you to feel pressured. I want things to work out with your family on Sunday, but I wanted you to know that there was another option in case it didn't."

"I don't know what's going to happen on Sunday, Chase. But I do know that I love you, and I want to be with you. And just knowing that you're here on this path with me, it's everything that I'll ever need."

I lean my forehead against hers. "And you by my side, that's all I'll ever need, too."

She smiles up at me and kisses me. "Everything's going to be okay," she affirms. I'm not sure if she's trying to convince herself or me.

I nod, "Yeah, it is."

"You promise that no matter what happens, even if they get really, really angry, you won't leave me?"

I lift her chin so that she's looking in my eyes. "I will never, ever leave you. I promise. No matter what happens, I will never, ever leave you. We will get through this together. You mean the world to me, future Mrs. Baker the baker." I add that last part to get a smile out of her and she rewards me with something even better, a laugh.

"I love you, Chase."

"I love you, too, baby girl."

# Chapter Twenty-One

The Monroe house is absolute chaos the morning of Ally and Alex's graduation. Mrs. Monroe is whipping through the house like a tornado, calling out orders and making sure everything is perfect for her twins' big day. I'm sitting in the living room with Trevor, Joey and Mr. Monroe, watching it all unfold. There's really nothing for us to do but stay out of the way. Alex was sitting with us, until his mother demanded he make himself presentable. She refused to go along with his idea to be naked under his gown, and insisted he wear a suit. He argued with her until they finally agreed on slacks and a button down, but she insisted on a tie and gave him "the look" until he caved.

And Ally. God, Ally looks gorgeous. She's wearing a knee-length navy dress with a dark red ribbon tied in an elegant bow around her waist, an homage to our high school's colors. Her sandy blonde hair is done in curls, spilling over her shoulders and down her back. She's positively glowing.

Once everyone is dressed, it's time for pictures. There are ones of Ally and Alex with and without their caps and gowns. There are pictures of them with their parents, with Trevor, and of the whole family together. Mrs. Monroe insists on getting shots of Alex with the band and of all the kids together. Ally convinces each of the guys to take an individual picture with her, I know this is so she'll have a picture with me from her graduation. It'll actually be our first real picture that isn't a selfie taken from one of our cell phones. I hope no one can detect the love, lust, and adoration in our eyes.

About an hour later, we're finally on our way to the school. The plan was for the ceremony to take place in the school's auditorium, but since the weather worked out, school officials went with their alternative plan of having it in the football stadium. The school is small, only about one hundred students per class, so the change works out without a hitch, and the stadium actually accommodates more people, so it won't be standing room only.

Ally and Alex are whisked away behind the scenes with the rest of their class, and

Trevor, Joey and I find a seat in the middle of the stands with Mr. and Mrs. Monroe. It isn't long before the commencement commences, and the guys and I are bored to tears by the faculty speeches.

I'm fidgeting in my seat, trying to pick out the back of Ally's head in the sea of navy blue caps up front, when Mrs. Monroe, who is sitting next to me, leans over and quietly says, "I see the way you look at her."

I freeze. I stop fidgeting, and I think I even stop breathing.

"You two are not as subtle as you think," she continues whispering. I look past her to Mr. Monroe and Trevor, and thankfully they're not paying us any attention. Wasn't looking forward to getting my ass kicked in the presence of all these people.

Not knowing how to respond, I just sit there. I can't confirm her findings, not without Ally. But I can't exactly ignore her either, that would be rude. This woman has been like a mother to me when my mother couldn't, or wouldn't.

I startle when she places her hand on my knee, I look to her and she's still facing forward, but she's smiling. "I love you like a son, Chase. I just want my daughter to be happy. You make her happy. Don't think I didn't notice how down she was after she and Blake broke up. She thinks she's good at hiding that stuff from me, but she's not. She did a complete one-eighty last summer and I know part of that was because of you. I know you'll take good care of her. You're a good boy." She removes her hand just as quickly as she had placed it there and continues watching the ceremony.

What the fuck just happened?

What do I say to that?

I can't just sit there and not say anything, so I say the only thing I can think of to let her know that I will do what she asks, I will take care of her. "I love her," I whisper. Out of the corner of my eye I see her smile widen.

"We know you do," she affirms.

"We?" I panic.

She turns to look at me and lets out a small laugh at the petrified look on my face. "Her father and I. You don't raise three teenagers without learning a trick or two." She winks.

I groan.

"I think it's almost over, man," Joey says from my left, squirming in his seat, assuming my groan meant that I'm as disgruntled about the length of the ceremony as he is.

I nod to him and turn back to Mrs. Monroe. "We were going to tell you."

"I'm sure you were," she smiles, patting my leg again.

"So Mr. Monroe isn't going to kill me?"

She stifles another laugh. "No. There will be no killing. Though I can't speak for Trevor and Alex," she grins. She has the same grin as Ally, or Ally has the same grin as her. Whatever. I just got the "all clear" from my secret girlfriend's parents, and I couldn't be happier. Not even death threats from Trevor and Alex could bring me down right now. I couldn't hide my smile if I tried.

"And now we present to you, our graduates," Principal Daniels states from the podium. We turn our attention to the front. Alphabetically, Ally and Alex are somewhere in the middle, so we've got a little ways to go.

"Jonathan Miller," he eventually says and Mrs. Monroe readies her camera, knowing Alex will be next. "Alexander Monroe," he says. We all whoop and holler as Alex walks across the stage and accepts his diploma. He gives a big grin and a wink to the crowd as he shakes the principal's hand. He steps off to the side, not leaving the stage just yet. I know he's waiting for Ally.

"Allyson Monroe," Principal Daniels calls. We whoop and holler again when Ally's name is called, Alex as well, startling Principal Daniels because he didn't realize he was waiting beside him. I smile as my girl takes her diploma and shakes his hand. Then laugh as Alex grabs her in a bear hug and spins her around. She swats at him, but I can tell she's laughing, too, loving that she gets to share this moment with him.

Mr. and Mrs. Monroe have tears in their eyes as they watch the scene. Trevor is holding his cell phone up, capturing video, I'm sure. And Mrs. Monroe hasn't stopped clicking on her camera. I'm sure they were probably like this when Trevor and I graduated, too.

The ceremony eventually wraps up, and Ally and Alex take pictures with some of their classmates. Mr. and Mrs. Monroe talk with some of the other parents, while Trevor, Joey and I hang out off to the side waiting on them.

"Where's dinner?" Joey asks, referring to the celebratory dinner we will be having after we get out of here.

"Where do you think?" Trevor sighs.

"Lombardi's," I supply.

"Figures," Joey laughs.

After Ally let Alex pick their birthday restaurant, she insisted that she get to choose their graduation restaurant. And Lombardi's it was. No one was surprised.

"Alright, you kids ready?" Mr. Monroe asks as he and Mrs. Monroe walk over, Alex and Ally trailing behind.

"Yeah," we three say together.

Mrs. Monroe laughs, "Hungry much?"

"Starving," Joey answers. He's always hungry.

"Come on, then," she wraps her arm around his shoulder and starts walking to the parking lot. "Ally and Alex, I want you to ride with us," Mrs. Monroe calls out. We rode in two cars because there wasn't enough room in one, and because we're planning to split up after dinner.

"Come on, Ma," Alex whines. "I want to ride with the guys."

"You're going to that party with the guys after dinner, you can ride with them then," she says. "I want my twinnies to ride with me."

"Just entertain your mother," Mr. Monroe nudges him.

"Alright," he agrees dramatically.

"We'll see you at the restaurant, drive carefully. Watch out for all these people," Mr. Monroe gestures towards the full parking lot.

"Got it, dad," Trevor says as we walk off to his car.

Before I follow him, I look over to Ally and catch her eye as she's talking animatedly to her mom. She smiles a small smile, and I smile back. Tomorrow can't come soon enough, I can't wait until our relationship is out in the open, so I can swoop in and hug her or kiss her whenever I want and no one will look at me like I'm crazy. Sure, I might get punched by her brothers, but at least I could hold her hand if I wanted to.

I can't believe her parents know! And why didn't they say anything sooner? Ally is going to be so relieved to know that. I can't wait to tell her. It will make the big reveal tomorrow that much easier.

"You coming, Baker?" Trevor calls.

I take one last, quick look at Ally. "Yeah," I call out and run to catch up with him and Joey.

"What was that about?" he asks once we're in the car. I'm riding shotgun and Joey's in the back, texting away on his phone.

"What's what about?" I play dumb.

"You were lingering."

"Sorry, just in a daze I guess."

He looks at me funny. "Everything okay?"

I could tell him. I could tell him right now and he might be okay with it. Trevor was always the levelheaded one. He might understand. He might even be able to cushion the blow of telling Alex. But I can't do that to Ally.

"Yeah, everything's fine. Just remembering our graduation. And hungry. Can't wait to eat."

He looks at me for another moment, then starts the car. "Me too, I'm starved."

I let out the breath I've been holding and relax back into my seat.

One more day. Just one more day.

***

The seven of us are seated at a table near the front of the restaurant, finishing up our dessert. I am sitting across from Ally, which is proving to be difficult. Every now and then her shoeless foot finds its way against my leg and causes me to nearly choke or spit out my drink. I tried to give her a stern look the first couple of times, but it was useless. Now I'm doing my best to ignore her.

Ally excuses herself to the restroom once she finishes her tiramisu, giving me a look and a slight nod of her head. I quickly look around to see if anyone else noticed, but they're all chatting and finishing their desserts.

I finish my cheesecake and excuse myself as well. The guys are none the wiser, but Mrs. Monroe has a small smirk on her face that leads me to believe she knows exactly what's going on. I don't know if I should be elated or completely weirded out about what she might be thinking.

I'm walking down the back hallway to the bathroom when I'm suddenly pulled into a dark service hallway. Next thing I know, Ally's arms are around my neck and her lips are on mine.

"Whoa," I say pulling back. "What's this?"

"I've been wanting to do that all day," she breathes out as she pulls me in for another kiss.

"Not that I'm not loving this," I say into her mouth. "But we can't be back here for long, you've already been gone for a few minutes. Might get suspicious." I think about telling her that her parents know about us, but she kisses me again, and I forget my own name.

"Today has been one of the best days ever," she sighs happily as she lays her head against my chest. "I'm so glad I got to spend it with you, even if I wasn't really with you."

"Yeah, nice going with the pictures."

She laughs, "I had to have at least one of us together."

"I'm glad you did it."

She leans up and kisses me again. "I wish I could go to the party with you guys."

"I know, baby girl. But you'll have a good time with Lucy. With you both going to separate schools in the fall, you won't get to spend much time together after the summer. But the guys and I will always be around."

"I know you're right. I'll just miss you tonight."

"I'll miss you, too."

"Don't get into any trouble," she warns.

"Who? Me?" I laugh. She knows as well as I do that I don't get into any trouble. Hell, none of us guys do. I barely drink at all, and the others may indulge in a celebratory beer or two, but we're all pretty mild when it comes to partying. We go for the music and to hang out with friends, possibly score gigs at other house parties. That's about it.

"I can't wait until I can go to those parties with you as your girlfriend."

I pull her in tight and hold her close to me. "You will."

"Soon?" she asks.

"Soon," I promise.

\*\*\*

When I return to the table a few moments later, the bill has been paid and everyone is getting ready to leave.

"Drop a deuce, man?" Joey asks.

"Ew, that's disgusting Joey," Ally cries.

I roll my eyes at him, "I got a phone call." He accepts the lie as truth, and we all head out of the restaurant.

"You boys behave yourselves and please don't stay out too late," Mrs. Monroe says as she gives us each a hug and a kiss on the cheek.

"No curfew tonight," Mr. Monroe says. "Be safe."

"You, too," Trevor calls out as he walks to his car.

"I love you all," Mrs. Monroe calls as she gets into their car.

"Love you, too," we all call back.

I wink at Ally as I get in the backseat, Alex is riding shotgun this time. I'm pretty sure she blew me a kiss in return, and I can't stop my grin. I don't even care if anyone saw.

"You ready to par-tay?" Alex calls out.

"Hell, yeah," Joey says and I nod.

"Let's do this," Trevor agrees.

I'm not really looking forward to the party, I'd much rather be with Ally and celebrate with her tonight. But it's Alex's night, too, and he wants to party. After tomorrow, I'll have the rest of my life to spend with Ally. Alex may hate me.

We pull out of the parking lot heading south, and in the rearview mirror, I watch the taillights of the Monroe's car with the love of my life, my Ally, heading north.

*Soon.*

# Chapter Twenty-Two

We're at the party for almost two hours before Alex gets a text from Lucy asking if he was still with Ally. I'm immediately on alert because I know Ally was heading straight over to Lucy's graduation party after dinner; her parents were supposed to be dropping her off there on their way home. She would have told Lucy if she had a change of plans.

"Did you try mom's cell phone?" Trevor asks Alex as we all step outside in the front yard.

"Yeah, hers and dad's. They both went to voicemail," Alex replies, looking worried.

"What about Ally's?" I ask, trying not to panic myself.

"Lucy tried her cell first, and I just tried it again."

"Let me try," I say and pull out my phone. Same thing, voicemail. I shake my head at them to let them know the call didn't go through. Why isn't she answering her phone?

"I just tried the house," Trevor says. "No answer."

"We better go look for them," Alex says and heads straight for the car. We all follow, saying nothing to anyone as we make our way down the street to where we parked. We get in the car, Trevor and Alex up front and Joey and I in the back.

"They probably got distracted on the way home, you know how Ally gets. Probably stopped for ice cream or something," Trevor tries to reason, but I can tell by the shakiness in his voice that he's starting to panic. He's just trying to hide it from his brother. As the oldest sibling, he's always trying to be stronger for the others.

"They had dessert at the restaurant," Alex says quietly. He's got his elbow propped up on the door and he's leaning his head into his hand. His hands are shaking, and he's completely freaking out.

"Maybe Ally wasn't feeling well and just went home and went to bed. She ate a lot at dinner. I've never seem someone so little pack in so much food," Joey offers. It's possible, but she still would have texted Lucy, or someone, to communicate the change in plans. She's meticulous about stuff like that for this very reason. She hates for people to worry. And why wouldn't their parents be answering their phones either? Or the house phone?

"I have a bad feeling," Alex says shaking his head.

We all whip our heads quickly to look at Alex. We know what he means when he says he has a bad feeling. He's had bad feelings before, once was when Ally fell out of their old treehouse and broke her arm, and the other time was the night she and Blake broke up. In both of those instances, his bad feeling was spot on.

"What kind of bad feeling?" I'm the first to ask.

"I don't know," he whispers.

"It's probably nothing," Trevor says.

"No," Alex says quietly. "It's not nothing. Pull over," he says quickly, "I'm going to be sick."

Trevor barely gets the car to the side of the road before Alex has the door open and is out of the car puking on the ground. He's on my side, so I get out and help him up.

"You alright, man?" I ask, knowing damn well that he's not okay.

When he looks up at me, I'm stunned to see tears running down his face. "I can't lose her, Chase. I can't." He drops his head and starts sobbing. My eyes widen, and I take a step back as I realize what he's saying.

He thinks he's going to lose her?

He can't lose her.

*I* can't lose her.

We're supposed to start our life together tomorrow, for real. Tomorrow is supposed to be the best day of our lives. It's supposed to be a new beginning. What am I supposed to do if she's not there?

Trevor gets out of the car and gets down on the ground with his brother. "We don't know that something bad happened. Let's just go to the restaurant and follow their route home. Maybe they just have a flat tire or something. You know that strip near Martin Road has shoddy cell reception and tons of pot holes."

Always the voice of reason. It makes me feel a little bit better myself, until I remember that they wouldn't have taken Martin Road to Lucy's house. But I don't say anything. I can't say anything. We all need to hang on to any hope we can.

Trevor helps Alex back into the car and Joey hands him a water bottle from the back seat. Alex rinses his mouth and spits the water out the open car door before shutting it.

"About an hour before I got the text from Lucy," Alex starts, "I had this sharp pain go straight through my body. It's the same feeling I had when Ally fell out of the tree, and when she and Blake broke up. I didn't think anything of it at the time, at any of those times, until after the fact when I realized she'd been in some kind of pain." He pauses for a moment and the car is completely silent. "I'm scared," he finally says.

Trevor reaches over and grabs Alex's hand. "We *will* find them," he says. He clearly knows better than to make promises he can't keep. Yes, we may find them, but will they be okay?

I sit back in my seat and look out the window. The sky is so cloudy, I can't see the moon.

***

We've been driving for about thirty minutes, following the route they would have taken from the restaurant back to the house. Then from the restaurant to Lucy's house. We don't see their car at all along the way at all, leaving us completely baffled as to what could have happened.

"Should we call the police?" Alex asks.

"What would we tell them? Our parents and sister are missing, help us find them? It's not exactly a kidnapping." Trevor sighs.

Alex nods. "Something just isn't right. What other way could they have gone?"

"Blanton's Bridge," I say quietly.

"What?" Trevor says.

"Blanton's Bridge," I say louder. "If there was traffic on the main road, your dad may have looped around to the bridge to enter Lucy's neighborhood from the back side. Which is very possible with all the graduations at the different schools today. There were probably a lot of people on the road."

Trevor's eyes widen as he takes a U-turn and heads back to the street that cuts through the middle of town and will lead us over to Blanton's Bridge Road. We're all completely silent as we weave through the dark streets, cautiously racing to the bridge.

My heart is racing, and in my mind and my heart, I'm praying to every deity out there that Ally and her parents are okay. As we round the bend before the bridge comes into view, my stomach sinks to the floorboards of the car.

"No. No, no, no, no!" Alex screams.

Trevor stops the car, and we all get out and run towards the emergency vehicles surrounding the entrance to the bridge.

"You can't come back here," a police officer standing just outside the barricade states.

"You don't understand, our parents and sister are missing. They may have come this way," Trevor tells him. "Please just let us see if it's their car down there."

A shadow seems to fall over the officer's face once Trevor mentions his parents and sister, and I just know. I just know it's them. I'm sure this officer knows enough about the occupants of the vehicle to know that they match Trevor's description.

"Look, son, just step on back, and I will have an officer come speak with you, okay?"

Trevor takes a step back, but Alex doesn't move.

"Come on, Al," Trevor says, pulling on his arm.

Alex doesn't leave his spot, he's staring down at the ground just beyond the police officer. I follow his gaze and freeze.

"We gave mom so much shit for that little tie-dyed monstrosity and refused to ride in the car with her so long as she had it on her antennae. Remember, Trev?" Alex says quietly as he looks at the small Mickey Mouse antennae ball on the pavement.

I look over at Trevor and he, too, is staring at it the small souvenir.

"We gave her such grief for it." A sob breaks free and Trevor pulls his little brother in his arms. "Why, Trev? Why did this happen to them?" Alex cries.

"I don't know," Trevor answers, his voice breaking. "I don't know."

Seeing my best friends, my brothers, falling apart causes my own tears to spill over.

*Ally.*

The police officer is still standing only a few feet away, watching the scene unfold, the brothers breaking in front of him. I take a brave step towards him. "Please," I beg. "Can you please tell us if they're still down there, if there were any...any survivors?" More tears spill down my cheeks, and my voice breaks as I say that last part.

The officer sighs, looks over to Trevor and Alex, then looks back at me. "Look, I'm in charge of traffic control, so I don't know what's going on down there," he gestures behind him. "But two ambulances have already left transporting victims to the hospital. Memorial General," he adds.

"Thank you," I tell him and step over to the guys. "Come on, we'll go to the hospital. The officer said ambulances have already brought people over. There's nothing we can do here, let's go, I'll drive."

The brothers seem strengthened by this information, and we all run back to the car and get in. I turn it around and head back to the main road, driving as carefully as I can despite the fact that I want to break every traffic law imaginable to get to the hospital. If they were taken away in an ambulance, that means they're alive, right?

# Chapter Twenty-Three

Because of the nature of the car accident, which I don't even want to begin to wonder about, the victims were brought in anonymously. Which means we can't get an update on anything until the police officers that were on the scene arrive with their identification. So we're just as clueless now as we were at the crash site.

It takes three hours before a police officer comes out and finds us in the waiting room of the emergency wing. "Monroe family?"

We all stand and Alex and Trevor approach the officer. Joey and I watch from behind as the officer speaks, trying to understand the range of emotions moving across Trevor and Alex's faces. First there's anger, then relief, then fear, then devastation. Total and complete devastation. The kind that can only come from losing someone you love.

As the officer walks away, Trevor and Alex fall into the seats directly behind them, tears pouring down their faces. Trevor puts his arm around Alex's shoulder and pulls him in. Joey and I get up and walk over. I need to know. I need to know if it's her. But I don't know how to ask. I can't find words.

Thankfully, Trevor speaks before I have to. "It was a drunk driver. Didn't wait for their car to finish crossing the bridge, just charged at them, tried to squeeze through I guess." This was the anger.

Alex leans forward in his seat and rests his head on his knees. Joey sits next to him and puts his hand on his back to let him know he's there.

"Dad," Trevor starts, then stops. He shakes his head as more tears flow. "He didn't make it. The car fell off the bridge and landed in the creek on his side. The officer said he died before they even got there; h-he drowned." And the devastation.

I look away. That man was a father figure to me. I don't even know how to process this.

"Mom is in really bad shape. She's in surgery. They say it doesn't look good. A lot of internal injuries." The fear.

"And Ally?" I rasp out, finally finding my voice.

"She has a couple broken bones and she hit her head pretty hard. She's unconscious, but that looks to be the extent of her injuries." And the relief. Oh God, the relief.

I breathe for what seems like the first time in hours. She's going to be okay. Ally is going to be okay. But how okay is she going to be if she comes through this without both of her parents? They were her world. They were all of our world. They were better parents to me and Joey than our own parents ever were.

I sit down on Trevor's other side as we wait for more news on his mom and Ally. An hour later, we find out their mom didn't make it. And three hours after that, we learn that Ally has a traumatic brain injury and is in a coma.

And just like that, the perfect world we were all living in just hours ago is completely shattered.

\*\*\*

The doctors convince us that there's nothing we can do at the hospital, so after confirming that they will call us if Ally's condition changes, we head home the following afternoon. It killed me to leave her there, but Trevor and Alex got to see her for a few minutes and said she looked peaceful. Bruised, but peaceful.

I drive us home, but later on, I don't even remember doing it. My mind is swarming with the events of the past twelve hours. We had gone from pure elation to total devastation. When we get to the house, Trevor and Alex invite Joey and me to crash on the couches. There's nowhere else I want to be. I feel closest to Ally here, in her home.

They retreat upstairs hoping to get some rest, though I'm not sure that they will. I'm not sure any of us will. Trevor and Alex just lost both of their parents, and their sister is comatose. The love of my life is comatose. I sink into the couch and close my eyes. Joey is already lying down on the other one. I don't know that I will sleep, but I need to try.

I'm lying there for about half an hour before I hear movement on the staircase. I know Joey's awake, too. We haven't spoken, but I can tell by his breathing and occasional sniffling that he's still awake. Case in point, he sits up as I do when the footsteps reach the bottom of the stairs.

Through the soft light of the lamp on the table beside the couch, I can just make out Trevor's shape as he rounds the corner at the bottom of the staircase. He looks up and catches my eye, then exhales and steps into the room. I move the useless pillows and blankets out of the way and Trevor sits beside me.

"I don't know what to do," he says after several moments of silence.

"There's not much you can do," I tell him, not knowing what else to say.

He nods and lays his head on the back of the couch, closing his eyes.

"I wish there was something I could do differently. That we all could have done differently, to make this night turn out a different way. Maybe if we didn't go to the party and followed them home. If Ally was with us, my parents probably wouldn't have ended up on that bridge."

"Yeah, or it might have been us that ended up on that bridge," Joey contributes.

Trevor sighs.

"There're a whole lot of 'what ifs,' Trev. If we could have known what was going to happen, we would have done everything differently. But we didn't, and we can't."

"I know, Chase. It doesn't make it any easier though."

We sit in silence for several minutes, and then hear Alex come down the stairs.

"Y'all couldn't sleep either?" he asks as he steps in the room and sits beside Joey on the other sofa. We all shake our heads in the negative. "Me either."

Eight lives changed tonight. The drunk driver who hit their car, killing Mr. and Mrs. Monroe and severely injuring Ally. He died himself. Then there's the four of us. Our lives will never be the same, Trevor and Alex more so than Joey and I, but it's all the same. Tomorrow, the next day, the day after that. It will all be different for us. No more Wednesday night dinners. No more late night phone calls and text conversations with Ally.

But at least she's alive. That's what I need to focus on. The good. Ally is alive. We will be together again someday.

At that moment, I remember that today is her birthday. It's supposed to be one of the happiest days of our lives. The first day of our future together.

*Happy birthday, baby girl.*

***

The funeral was full of distant relatives, friends, business associates of Mr. and Mrs. Monroe, and friends of Trevor, Alex, and Ally. One of the partners at Mr. Monroe's firm and his wife, Steve and Laurie Adelson, close friends of the Monroes, helped Trevor and Alex with the arrangements. Mr. Adelson was also the one who prepared Mr. and Mrs. Monroe's estate, so he helped with the execution of their will as well.

Mr. and Mrs. Monroe were both only children, and their parents had passed away years before, so they had no immediate relatives. No one to step in and play parents to Trevor and Alex. Not that it mattered since they were both adults now, and no one could ever replace their parents.

Everything was left to their children, and Trevor and Alex saw to it that something was set up for Ally so she could receive her benefits when she woke from the coma. The house was paid off, so they decided that's where they would stay. They wanted Ally to have something familiar to come home to and they weren't ready to part with the last remaining connection to their parents.

Two weeks went by and Ally didn't wake up. After the third week, the hospital transferred her into a long-term care facility. Trevor and Alex visited her every day, and I visited as often as I could without them getting suspicious. I couldn't find it in me to tell them about our relationship without Ally. We had always planned to tell them together, and that's how it would stay.

Two months after the accident, we return to our gig at the restaurant near the airport. They were happy to have us back, Mr. Monroe's friend was extremely understanding regarding our break, and our small following was thrilled. Everyone extended their sympathies for our loss, and we really rocked our first night back. We played that first show back for Mr. and Mrs. Monroe, and for Ally, and it was probably the best one we ever did.

# Chapter Twenty-Four

I get off work early one Wednesday afternoon because of the rain, and decide to take advantage and visit Ally. Trevor and Alex will still be at work, so I know I won't bump into them there. This has become sort of a tradition. Any time it rains and the construction site closes, and I get off early, I visit Ally.

On these days, I talk to her for hours. I tell her about my days, I tell her how much I miss her. I tell her how beautiful she still is and how much I will always love her. Some days I just lay my head on her bed, hold her hand and cry. I cry for what she's lost, for what we've lost. I cry because she has no idea, no idea what's happened.

Today, I'm bringing my guitar with me. I wrote a song for her. I don't usually write lyrics, and I don't know that she can really hear me, but I'm still nervous.

I pull the light blue, faux suede arm chair up to her bedside and unpack my guitar. I pluck a few strings, making sure it's tuned right, as I get myself situated. Then I begin.

*Lying here with you,*

*It's better than I imagined it would be.*

*Waiting here with you,*

*How worthwhile I know it will be.*

*Under our moon,*

*Promises made.*

*Under our moon,*

*A love I wish had stayed.*

*Now you're gone,*

*But not that far away.*

*You'll come back,*

*It's all I ever pray.*

*Under our moon,*

*Promises made.*

*Under our moon,*

*A love I wish had stayed.*

*I'm left here missing you,*

*And no one understands.*

*The pain I feel every day,*

*It's all in someone else's hands.*

*Under our moon,*

*Promises made.*

*Under our moon,*

*A love I wish had stayed.*

*Baby, come back to me,*

*And happy we will be.*

*Baby, please,*

*Please just find your way,*

*Until then, forever yours I will stay.*


I rest my cheek on the bed beside her, looking up at her face. I will her to wake up and to open her eyes. I would give anything, even my own life, just to look into her beautiful blue eyes again.

"That was beautiful," a voice says from behind me, and I jump up. It's just one of the nurses. The younger, nicer one. "I'm sorry," she says quietly. "I didn't mean to startle you."

"It's okay," I say, wiping the tears I didn't realize had escaped. "It's just always so quiet around here."

"It is," she nods. "Did you write that?" she asks as she checks Ally's stats.

"Yeah. Is she okay?" I ask, concerned.

"The same," she replies as she takes down some notes. I nod and begin to pack up my things. "You don't have to go, visiting hours aren't over yet."

"I know, I just have to get out of here before her brothers stop by." She looks at me a little strangely. "They don't know about us," I tell her. "We never got the chance to tell them."

She nods sadly, "I understand. I won't say anything if I see them, but they could always check the visitor's log."

"We're all best friends, so it's okay if they know I came. It's just if they knew how...personal...the visits are..."

She nods, "Fair enough."

"Thanks," I say to her. Then I turn back to Ally and kiss her forehead. "I love you, baby girl."

As I walk past the nurse on the way out, I swear I see tears in her eyes.

One of the interesting things about playing a restaurant near the airport is that you just never know who is going to walk through the door. Once in a while, we've seen actors who are vacationing or filming nearby. Occasionally it's musicians and their suits who are passing through town on tour.

Tonight, it's the tour manager for one of the hottest bands on the radio right now, Infrared Flamingos. Apparently he loved our set and they just had one of their opening bands drop out of the tour back in Maryland.

"I'd like to talk to the execs about you guys, got a manager?"

"No, man," I tell him. "Trevor here handles our bookings and finances."

"The label could probably hook you up with someone for the tour, if they decide they want you. A temporary thing, just so you could just focus on the music and let someone else handle the business side of things."

Trevor nods, "Sounds good." The tour manager, Bill, gets Trevor's number and tells him he'll be in touch within the week.

Turns out we didn't have to wait that long at all. Bill called back two days later, on Monday, and said the execs loved the clip he had recorded on his phone and played for them. They wanted to fly us up to New York to hear us in person and go over the tour contract. We ask Mr. Adelson, Mr. Monroe's old partner, to join us since we don't know a thing about contracts.

"This all looks legit," Mr. Adelson says as he finishes reading the last page. "Just show up for the shows, stay out of trouble, and you're all set."

Our audition went off without a hitch, and the suits loved us. Said we were just what they were looking for, both for the tour and possibly the label. They quickly corralled us in a conference room and handed over stacks of paperwork.

"What about transportation?" Trevor asks.

"We've room on one of our buses. You'd have to bunk with other bands, but it beats having to come up with your own ride," one of the execs tells us.

"Can we have a minute to discuss it privately?" Trevor asks him.

"Absolutely," the exec says and they all step out.

"I'll be right outside," Mr. Adelson says as he gets up and follows them out.

"So what do you guys think?" Trevor asks.

"It sounds awesome," Joey says.

"Yeah," Alex nods, but I can tell something is holding him back. The same thing that's probably holding me back, and Trevor.

"What about Ally?" I ask.

Trevor looks at me, relief that someone else is thinking about where she fits into this is clear on his face. "I don't want to leave her, but she would want us to do this, right?"

I think about it for a minute, and decide that yes, Ally would want us to do this. She would be over the moon for us. "Yeah, she definitely would."

"She would be pissed if we didn't," Joey adds.

"Hell, yeah, she would," Alex agrees.

"And look at the tour stops," Trevor points. "Several of them are on the east coast. There's opportunity to stop by and visit with her."

"But what if something happens with her condition and we have to come back? What if we have to break the contract?" I ask.

Trevor sighs. "Maybe we can talk to them? Explain our situation beforehand and see if they'll give us any flexibility for a family emergency."

"Doesn't hurt to try," I say.

We call Mr. Adelson and the remaining suit back in the room, and Trevor doesn't waste any time. "Look, we have a family commitment tying us to Charlotte. Our sister," he gestured to himself and Alex, "is in a coma. If anything changes with her condition, we're going to need to be there. We want you to know that we're taking this offer very seriously, but our parents just died, and she's all we have left. And we're all she has left. She's the most important thing to us right now, to all of us. We can't sign anything that prevents us from going to her if she needs us. And we're not going to sign anything that penalizes us for doing that either."

Mr. Adelson looks impressed with Trevor's speech, but the suit remains expressionless. The room is silent for a full minute before he finally speaks. "Your attorney here was just telling me a bit about you boys and your character while we were standing outside. Said you're upstanding young men, never get into trouble, and that family was, is, important to you. He mentioned you had a recent tragedy and might not be willing to leave the area for a prolonged period of time. In fact, he said he was surprised you were entertaining the idea of a tour at all."

Well, this isn't the direction we were hoping this would go. It sounds like the guy is about to rescind the offer. Thanks a lot, Adelson.

"But," he starts back up and he has our undivided attention, "you have an impressive talent. We want you on this tour, and we will do just about anything to get you on it. Think of it as a long-term audition. If we like what we see, you may just get a record deal out of it."

We look at each other like we can't believe what we're hearing. First a tour, then a record deal? But he still hasn't addressed our concern. What happens if Ally needs us?

"As for the tour, we will need a contract. That's non-negotiable in business, as I'm sure you can expect. But I'm sure our legal department can work in some kind of 'escape clause' pertaining to your sister. So what do you say? We got a deal?"

We look at each other, able to read each other's' facial expressions after spending so much time together.

"Yeah, we've got a deal," Trevor says for the group as he steps forward to shake the man's hand.

"Good," he smiles as he shakes the rest of our hands. "I will have our legal team revise the contract immediately, and I will have it back to you to review within the hour. Why don't you head on down to the cafeteria and have lunch and meet me back up here afterwards?"

"Sounds good, sir. Thank you," Trevor, our apparent spokesperson, says.

We float down in the elevator on a cloud. We're going on tour. We're going on tour with an awesome band that we idolize. We could get signed to a label, to their label. After the absolute hell we've experienced over the past three months, things are finally starting to look up. If only Ally was awake to enjoy the ride with us.

# Chapter Twenty-Five

"It's going to be amazing," I say as I sit at Ally's bedside, holding her soft hand, rubbing my thumb across her knuckles. "We're going to get to visit places we never thought we ever would and always dreamed we could. The only thing that will be missing is you. I know I have to do this, for the guys, for you, for your parents. We owe it to you guys, to ourselves. But I don't know how to do it without you. I'm going to miss seeing your face, holding your hand, and singing to you. I love you so much, baby girl."

We signed the tour contract and will meet up with the rest of the bands in South Carolina tomorrow. Trevor and Alex came by to say goodbye to Ally this morning, and I lied and told them I had some stuff I wanted to grab from my mom's apartment this afternoon, but I was really coming here. I needed to imprint her face, the feel of her skin, and her smell in my memory for the six months we will be gone. I'm not sure how I'll be able to squeeze in visits at the same time Trevor and Alex are trying to squeeze in visits.

God, I hope she wakes up soon. As much as I want to live out this dream with the band, I want Ally to be by my side even more. If I had to give it all up for her, I would. We all would. Hence the escape clause in the contract.

I lean in and kiss her forehead, my usual parting gift. "I love you, baby girl. And I will see you real soon. We'll make you proud, Ally. We'll make you so proud."

As I'm walking out, I give the nurse, Amy, the same one who was there the day I sang to Ally that first time, my phone number. "Please call or text me if anything happens. I know y'all have her brothers' contact information, but if you can't reach them. Please try me."

She nods and smiles. "Good luck, Chase."

"Thanks, Amy."

***

I head back to the house to finish packing my stuff. I never left the Monroes' after the accident; I kind of made a home on the couch. It was where I felt closest to Ally, and I just couldn't bring myself to be anywhere else. Trevor and Alex appreciated the company, as well. And Joey crashed on the couch most of the time, too.

Eventually, Trevor offered us the attic above the garage. It was unfinished, but he knew I had the construction skills to finish it, so I did. There was already plumbing out there because of the bathroom in our practice area downstairs, so it didn't take much to turn it into a fully functional apartment. I was pretty pleased with the results, as were Trevor and Alex. It raised the property value if they ever chose to sell it.

I'm in the apartment packing when Trevor comes up. "You almost packed?" he asks.

"Yep, just finishing up."

"I can't believe we're doing this," he says as he sits on one of the bar stools in the kitchenette.

"I know, it's surreal."

"I wish mom and dad could see us now, and Ally. They'd all be so excited."

I nod, "Your mom and dad *can* see us now, and I bet they're excited. They're probably running around telling everyone they know up there all about their boys going on the road." Trevor laughs, and I imagine he's picturing just that, his mom running around telling anyone who will listen that her boys are in a band, and they're going on tour.

She probably even has her camera in her hand.

"I wish Ally was coming with us," he says solemnly.

"Me too," I say. And he has no idea how much.

"She named us, you know? It's like she has been a part of the band since the beginning. I loved it when she started coming around again last summer. Alex did, too. It was like old times again."

"She'll be around again, it will be like old times again," I affirm. She has to, there's just no other option.

"I really miss her. I never thought of her as a brat or an annoying little sister, you know?" I nod, though it was rhetorical. Trevor just needs to talk. He needs an outlet. Leaving this place after the accident without Ally isn't easy for any of us. "I hope she knows that. I hope she knows how special she was... is... will always be."

I sit down beside him, "She knows. You and Alex are like her best friends. There's no one she would rather spend time with."

Trevor nods, "I know you're right. Just sucks she's not doing this with us."

"She'll catch the next one," I say, willing it to be true.

Trevor smiles, "She will, won't she?"

"Yeah. When we come back and tell her about it, she'll be so pissed she missed it that she'll wake right up," I laugh, "hell bent on making the next one."

"That's Ally, for sure," he agrees. "It feels good to talk about her. Alex is just so fucked up about it. He can't talk about her. I mean I get they have the whole twin connection thing, but I just wish he would talk instead of keeping it bottled up inside."

"I'm sure he'll loosen up some on the tour. Being here in the house can't be easy."

"You're right," he stands up. "I'm going to finish packing. I'll see you in the morning."

"See you in the morning."

*** 

So far, the tour has been amazing. We've gotten to spend a lot of time with some of the other opening acts, like Challenge Demands and 12 Inches Limp. Yes, that's their name. No, I'm not kidding. And no, I don't know if it's true. This isn't their first tour, so it's nice to hear stories of their experiences. The guys from Infrared Flamingoes are pretty awesome, too. They don't hang out with us too much because they're always running around for interviews and other publicity stuff, but considering they're extremely famous, they're still pretty humble and hang out with the little people from time to time.

The living arrangements on tour aren't that bad. We're on a double decker bus that sleeps fourteen upstairs in very narrow bunks, and has a small kitchen and several lounge spaces downstairs. 12 Inches Limp and Challenge Demands are on the bus with us, along with a few roadies that didn't fit on the roadie bus. There's an XBOX, Playstation, and satellite TV set up in each of the lounge areas, so it's really like a home away from home. If we stay in a place for more than a night, the label hooks us up with hotel rooms for the night. We have to double up, but at least it gives us the opportunity to stretch our legs and escape the cabin fever of the bus.

Alex and Joey are happier than pigs in shit over all the girls at each of the stops. Trevor indulges once in a while, but usually ends up hanging out with me on the bus or in the hotel. He doesn't ask me why I'm not partaking in all the willing bodies, which is good, because I could never tell him that I'm holding off for the girl I love back home. Who's in a coma. Who also happens to be his sister. Yeah, that wouldn't go over well at all.

The label was so impressed with our performances and our professionalism on tour that they offered us a record deal after only five shows. We had Mr. Adelson look over the record contract, and he said it looked solid. It requires us to do three albums in three years, and at least two more six month tours. We made sure that our "Ally clause" was in there and signed on the dotted line.

We also negotiated the use of a Charlotte studio to record our albums, part of our "Ally clause," and as soon as we get back to town, we will begin recording our first album. We already have several original songs, so we plan to use some of our favorites that the label approves of, and write a few new ones. I think about using "Our Moon," the song I wrote for Ally, but it's just too personal. I'm not ready to share something so intimate with the world.

***

When we return to Charlotte after the tour, we're plus one. Joey met the love of his life, Evie, in Dallas about two weeks in and they got hitched on our tour stop in Vegas. It was totally insane, but totally Joey, and I have to say that the two of them are perfect for each other and so happy together. It's also pretty cool for me because now I get the apartment to myself since they're moving in together.

We hit the studio almost immediately, and our first single, "Fall Down," is a huge hit with tons of airtime. We spend some time in New York and L.A. doing radio interviews and attending award shows. Who would have thought that not even a year after meeting Bill at the restaurant that all this would have happened?

I steal visits with Ally in between studio time. I can't believe she hasn't woken up yet. The doctors are still optimistic and always comment positively about her brain activity.

But still, I never would have imagined that eleven months after the accident, Ally would still be asleep.

# Chapter Twenty-Six

"Take five, then we'll put it all together," Jerry, the sound guy at the recording studio, calls over the speaker.

I set down my guitar and raise my hands over my head to stretch. We've been at it all day, laying down the first couple of tracks for our second album. My arms and fingers are almost numb. The rest of the guys are doing the same thing, stretching and shaking out their hands and arms.

I wouldn't change a thing though because we are on point today. Ever have one of those days where everything is going right? The sun is shining, birds are chirping and all that shit? Well, today is that day. We nailed two songs already this morning, each in under two takes. It's a beautiful day.

So yeah, I might not be able to feel my fingers, but when you've got something good going like that, you don't quit. And I can tell all the guys are feeling it, too. We're all humming with the energy. None of us can really sit still, and I'm glad this break will be a short one because I'm already ready to get back to it.

I had no idea it was all about to get better.

We step outside of the recording room to grab some water, hot tea for Alex to soothe his throat, and a snack, and to check our phones for messages and do the whole social media thing. I down half of my water bottle in one swallow as I go through the notifications on my phone. One of the label's marketing people recommended we each have our own social media pages – Facebook, Twitter, and Instagram – to keep in touch with our fans. It's fun, but it takes forever to sort through everything and determine what to respond to. It's impossible to respond to everything, but I'd hate to piss off a fan. After all, they made us what we are today. I just wish I could filter out all the spam.

Halfway through my notifications, I see a missed call from a local, unknown number and a few text messages from that same number.

| **Unknown:** | Call me!! |
| **Unknown:** | It's Amy. |
| **Unknown:** | The nurse. |

My heart thumps in my chest. Ally. Is she awake?

Before I can tap to call her, a loud cheer breaks out behind me, and I turn to see Alex down the hallway, jumping on Trevor's back, smiling like someone just told him the McRib was back.

Or that his sister is awake.

*She's awake.*

Trevor is on the phone, shaking Alex off his back, but he's smiling, too.

I step over to Joey and nudge his shoulder. "What's going on?" I ask, already knowing what the answer is and damn near ready to jump out of my skin and get to the long-term care center where Ally is.

He shrugs. "Not sure. But by the looks on their faces, I think it has something to do with lil' sis." He looks at me and smiles wide; I match his expression with a big smile of my own.

Best. Day. Ever.

\*\*\*

After quickly explaining the situation to Jerry, we hightail it out of the studio and pile into Trevor's SUV.

"We need to call Humph," Alex says, bouncing in the front passenger seat.

"I got it," I tell him. I pull my phone out of my pocket and see the text from Nurse Amy still up on the screen. I type out a quick text telling her we're on our way, then find Humphrey Morris in my contacts and tap to call.

Turns out the suit/exec/label guy had a name. Humphrey Morris. He was apparently born to be an executive with that given name. Poor guy. He's actually really cool, though. He kind of took us all under his wing and treats us like his kids. Probably doesn't hurt that we don't ever give him any shit.

"Morris," his gruff voice stated.

"Hey, Humph," I say. "It's Chase."

"Chase! To what do I owe the honor? Heard you boys are doing a bang up job in the studio today." I could hear the smile in his voice. I'm positive we're his favorite band to work with, but he would never admit that. No matter how many times Alex and Joey have asked. It would be like a parent admitting who their favorite child was.

"Yeah, we're having a great day. And it just got a hell of a lot better."

"Oh yeah?" he says curiously.

"Escape clause," I tell him. We've taken to referring to Ally as "escape clause" when we're around Humph. He actually started it, always taking a moment to ask how our "little escape clause" was doing.

He's silent for a moment, then says, "She's awake?"

I can't help the excited laugh that comes out. "Yeah, man! She's awake!"

"That's excellent news!" he shouts. And I know he means it. He's not the derisive type; he genuinely cares. And no, I'm not naïve; he does actually care. His secretary even told us once that she's never seen him take to a group like he did to us. She said it's because we respect him, cause no trouble, and genuinely love what we do.

"We're on our way to the facility now, and we probably won't know much until after the guys talk with the doctors, but we will let you know what's going on as soon as we find out."

"Take all the time that you need," he assures. "Well, not too much time," he laughs. "You're already ahead of schedule with the album since you guys work so damn hard, so you've got some breathing room. Do what you've got to do, just keep me in the loop."

"Will do. Thanks a lot, Humph."

"Don't worry about it. Give Trevor and Alex a high five for me, or a fist bump or whatever the hell it is you kids do these days."

I laugh, "I'll do that. Thanks again."

"Yep," and he hangs up. That's just Humph. He never says goodbye. The first few times any of us spoke with him over the phone, we all thought he hated us. The manager the label had appointed us for the tour, Pompous Thomas, rolled his eyes and told us Humphrey Morris did that to everyone. We never did like Thomas very much and were happy to see him replaced with someone more easy-going after the tour was over.

*** 

Joey and I are sitting in the waiting room at the facility, waiting for word from Trevor and Alex. They've been back with the doctor for over an hour already and I'm starting to get antsy. It's a typical hospital-type waiting area with one television set to news and the other to a soap opera. To avoid going crazy, you can read a magazine or play on your phone.

"Dude, chill out. What's your problem?" Joey asks, and I realize I must really be wigging out if *Joey* tells me to chill out. But I can't help it. What if Ally asks for me? What if she tells them about us? Oh man, and what if they tell her about their parents? She's going to be devastated.

I stop my pacing and sit in the seat one over from Joey. "Sorry, man. They've been back there a while."

"She has been asleep for a year, bro." He laughs as he flips through a *Better Homes & Gardens* magazine. "They have a lot to catch up on."

I hope that's all it is.

Another hour later, and I'm trying to beat level ninety-four of *Candy Crush*, when I hear footsteps. I look up to see Trevor and Alex walking into the waiting room. Taking note of their ominous expressions, Joey and I jump up to meet them.

"What's going on?" I ask. "She's okay, right?"

Alex, looking utterly lost, looks to Trevor. This isn't good. Alex was flying high when we walked in this place a couple hours ago. What the fuck happened back there?

"She doesn't remember us," Trevor says flatly. "She's got amnesia."

And just like that, the bottom drops right back out.

# Chapter Twenty-Seven

Five weeks. Ally has been awake for five weeks, and I haven't been able to seen her one time. Trevor and Alex go to the rehab center for therapy sessions with her and to visit. After a rough first week, they say she's doing well and opening up, but still nothing on the memory front. Which means I'm the only person in the world who knows how much I love her, and how much she loves me. Or loved me. I don't know what to think anymore.

If it's possible, I feel like I miss her more now that she's awake than I did while she was asleep. Knowing she's there and awake and I can't see her or touch her, it's a whole different kind of pain. It's the pain of the love of your life living her life without you. Even if she doesn't know any better, it still sucks. Sucks for her. Sucks for me. It sucks for all of us that she's not the same Ally she was a little more than a year ago. But I have faith that she's still in there somewhere, and she'll find her way back to us. To me.

The good news? She's coming home today. I will finally get to see her. Even if I can't hold her and tell her how much I love her, I'll get to see her perfect face and hopefully, that beautiful smile I miss so much.

***

Acting like a peeping Tom just inside my apartment window, I catch a too brief glimpse of Ally when they first arrive at the house, and damn if it didn't make my heart hurt. It has been too long since I've seen her up and moving about. She looks good. Healthier than when I last saw her, asleep at the facility. The rehab and exercise she has been getting has been good to her. But she seems to sort of break down when she gets out of the car, and it takes everything I have to not rush down there and hold her.

I know it's a dick move, but I decide to head out to the backyard to catch a better look at her. I can't stop myself if I try. I know Trevor wants to wait until she's a little more comfortable at home before introducing her to people, but when I heard them splashing in the pool, I couldn't resist. It's like there's a magnet pulling me to her, and no force can stop it.

I step into the backyard and try to stop my eyes from immediately gravitating towards Ally, but again, I can't stop the force. She's lying on an inner tube near where Alex is shooting hoops into the poolside net. I make my way over to Trevor by the grill, with the ruse of speaking to him about a conversation I had earlier today with Humph. It isn't a complete lie. I did talk to Humph today, but it could have waited.

"Hey, man," I say as I approach. "Sorry, I didn't realize she was out here," I begin, tipping my head towards the pool. "Figured she would be inside settling in."

Trevor nods in my direction, "It's all good. What's up?"

"Spoke to Humph this morning," I start.

"'Bout what?"

"Getting back in the studio," I say.

"Yo, Baker!" Alex shouts from the pool.

I pause my conversation with Trevor and look over to the twins. Ally lifts her head and looks at me, I can't see her eyes because of the sunglasses she has on, but I can still tell she's looking at me. I smirk and watch as her creamy skin turns pink in a blush.

Yep, caught you. My smirk deepens. It's good to know that her memory loss doesn't seem to have affected the fact that her body wants me. It still wants me. I do an internal fist pump.

Trevor shakes his head. "What were you saying about Humph?"

"Right," I say turning back to him. "He said he'll give us more time, if we need it, to get Ally settled. But he would like for us to try to get back in the studio, even if only for a few hours a week, as soon as possible."

I'm trying to look at Trevor while he's speaking, but I can't help but glance over to Ally every few seconds. She looks so peaceful lying there, much like she did while she was in the coma. It both pleases me and pains me to see her like that. It's pleasing because I know she's not really sleeping, she's awake and relaxing, maybe even enjoying herself. It's painful because I want to see her eyes open, I want to hear her speak and laugh. I want to watch her swim and walk and talk. I don't want to see her sitting still any longer. One year was long enough.

Trevor sighs, and I look back to him. "Yeah, I guess we can do that. I mean he has done a lot for us, I don't want to make it seem like we're trying to take advantage. I'm sure we can swing a few hours here and there. Let's regroup about it in a couple days."

I nod, "Sounds good." We continue to discuss ideas on some songs for the new album, ones that will sync well with the tracks we've already laid down. We wrote a lot of music before we got signed, so we have quite the catalogue to choose from.

Splashes and shrieks from the pool catch mine and Trevor's attention. We look over to see a soaking wet Ally yelling at a laughing Alex. "Some things never change," I say just as she looks up at me.

"Got that right," Trevor laughs.

Trevor and I finish our discussion about band stuff, and I'm getting ready to excuse myself when Joey and Evie show up. I watch with a mixture of wonder, alarm, and envy as he jumps right in the pool and hugs her. If it wasn't so completely out of character for me to do that, I would have. Dammit, I should have anyway. I watch Ally closely, as does Trevor and Alex, looking for any sign of alarm or reservation from her, but there's none. Joey is harmless and it seems she knows it. I can't help but smile at the warm exchange between Joey and Ally. She's the missing piece. Our missing piece. My missing piece. And now we're all whole again. Well, almost whole.

I hear her laugh and say, "You have all your clothes on!" God, she has a beautiful laugh and it's so good to hear it.

"Not the first time, won't be the last." I find myself saying, just wanting to interact with her in some way other than stolen glances. She looks at me again, and our eyes connect briefly, just long enough for me to spot the blush on her cheeks.

I help Trevor cook the steaks on the grill, participating intermittently in conversation as Evie corrals Joey so they can leave for her doctor's appointment. I want what they have. Again, I can't help but be envious. A year ago, I could see that in my future. Maybe not my immediate future since Ally is so young, but eventually. Life sure has a funny way of working out.

"Hey, man, want to stay for dinner?" Trevor asks as he plates the last of the steak to bring in the house.

"Sure, thanks." Trevor nods and steps passed me into the house. We three usually ate dinner together, but tonight would be different. For the first time in over a year, Ally would be dining with us. My Ally. And it's Wednesday, how about that.

As usual, my gaze finds her as I follow Trevor into the house and I stop for a moment. She's back to floating on her inner tube, sunglasses on, face tilted towards the sky. I take in every inch of her beautiful body, from the tip of her toe to the top of her head, focusing a little too long on those ruby red lips I used to love to kiss. I wonder if they taste the same. As I look up to her eyes, I realize she's looking at me. Busted.

# Chapter Twenty-Eight

*Present*

Everyone was quiet for a beat after I finished my perspective on the last two years of our life–my life. My life with Ally. My life without Ally. Ally coming back into my life. I didn't want to tell her all this in front of them. I wanted to share it with her privately. But with the way everything went down, I didn't know what the hell else to do.

"Dude, you're a virgin?" Joey finally says, breaking the deafening silence.

I laugh. "That's all you got from that?"

"Sorry, man," he shrugs. "Evie always says I'm a twelve year old boy trapped in a man's body."

"You son of a bitch!" Alex roars as he jumps off the couch. Trevor quickly gets up and stands in his way as he tries to get to me. "You were screwing around with our sister behind our backs?" Alex yells.

And there it is, the freak out I knew would eventually happen when all was revealed. Alex is usually a pretty laid-back dude, but when someone messes with his family, all bets are off. Pile on the fact that I probably just refreshed his emotions of losing his parents and nearly losing Ally, and he has the potential to be a very loose cannon. Out of the corner of my eye, I see Ally take a step back at Alex's outburst, and I instinctively stand from my seat and put myself between him and her. The movement only irritates Alex more.

"It wasn't like that, man. I swear." I'm not just defending myself, but Ally as well. Eventually Alex will realize it was both of us hiding stuff from everyone and I don't want him to turn his anger on her.

"Dude, chill out," Trevor says to Alex and pushes him back to the couch to sit.

"Alex, come on, man. We're all family here, he wouldn't do that. He wouldn't hurt Ally," Joey tries to reason. At least someone seems to be on my side. Trevor is looking at me like I'm a stranger, Alex looks like he wants to kill me, and Ally... Ally just looks defeated.

Alex laughs. "Right. Did either of you just hear what he said? They were running around behind our backs for months." I don't miss how he says "they" that time, and my heart hurts for Ally. She doesn't deserve this. I knew it then, and I know it now, but dammit, I love her.

Trevor and Joey look like they're considering what Alex is saying, and Ally is just looking at me with the saddest eyes I've ever seen. "I'm sorry I didn't tell you, baby girl," I whisper. "So sorry."

She's standing there, frozen, at the edge of the room. Her eyes jerk from mine, to the others before she collapses on the floor. Her breaths are coming in pants, and I know she's having an anxiety attack.

I rush over to her and rub my hand in soothing circles on her back. Whispering reassuring words, trying to calmly guide her breathing. This worked when she had the one in the kitchen a while ago, and I hope she's not too upset with me to let it work now.

"Get your fucking hands off her!"

"Alex, back off! You're not helping!" Trevor says.

"I'm okay," she whispers after a few minutes of deep, labored breathing. She unfolds herself from her protective position on the floor. I shuffle back and help her to stand.

"Here, let's get you over to the chair." I say to her. With my hand on her elbow, I guide her to the chair I had vacated a few minutes ago and let her sit down, then I hand her my water bottle. Hopefully, she doesn't mind that I already drank out of it.

"Thank you," she says quietly, looking down at the bottle in her hands.

"You're welcome." I smile sadly and take her place in the center of the room. "Look, I know you're all pissed," I start, making eye contact with everyone in the room. "And I get that. If I thought someone was hurting Ally, I'd be freaking out, too. But it wasn't like that."

"You were messing around with my sister. You both lied to us. To all of us." Alex snarls. Trevor is still standing in front of him, and Joey is ready to pounce should Alex try to get up again.

Finally, Trevor moves from his position guarding Alex and approaches me. I tense, not knowing what to expect, but then Trevor surprises me by pulling me into a hug. "Why the hell didn't you say something after the accident? Her being in a coma, waking up and not remembering, it had to be killing you."

I pull away and look Trevor right in the eyes. "It was hard. But I couldn't tell you without her. We promised we'd do it together.

She means the world to me, and I couldn't break that promise. Even if that meant that I had to hold back my true feelings about everything."

Trevor nods. "Look, I don't know what's going to happen since she doesn't remember anything. But I support you guys." He looks over to Ally when he says that last part. Then he looks back at me. "But if you do one damn thing to pressure her or hurt her—"

"I would never," I interrupt, knowing that's a lie because I already hurt her by starting something with her again and withholding the truth. "I've prayed every day after the accident that she would come back to us. And I've prayed every day since she's woken up that she'll eventually find her way back to me." I turn my attention to Ally and plead my case, "I know this is all a lot to take in, and it's why I never said anything. I didn't want to confuse you or make you think you had to feel something you didn't. I knew that eventually you'd either find your way back to me on your own, or you'd remember. We hadn't been in love long before, but it was strong, and I have had no doubt that one day, it will pull us back together again."

And it did. It did pull us back together again. And now my stupidity just might be tearing it back apart.

Alex, who has remained silent since his last outburst, finally gets up from his spot on the couch. He glares individually at each person in the room. "This is fucked up. They both lied to us. I don't give a shit what the circumstances were. We *were* a family, and they lied," he points in mine and Ally's direction. He doesn't raise his voice; he just states it all solemnly.

"Alex," Ally starts.

"No. I'm trying to cut you some slack now because you don't know what the hell you did back then, but I'm not going to be quiet anymore. This is messed up. I'm your twin, damn it. We might not have always been the best of friends, but senior year we were tight. And you didn't say anything."

He is hurt. He is hurt, and I couldn't blame him because he's right to feel that way. I hate that he's hurting Ally, because I feel like she is an extension of myself, but what can I do that won't make it worse?

"But," she tries again.

"No, Ally. Just no." He looks over at Trevor. "He's supposed to be your best friend and he kept something this big from you, and you're just accepting it?" He shakes his head. "I'm out of here."

"Alex," Trevor calls after him. Alex doesn't turn around; he just keeps walking out of the room and a few seconds later we hear the front door slam shut, the loud bang causing Ally to jump.

"He'll come around," Trevor says.

"Well, I'm gonna head home. Let you guys talk," Joey says. He walks over to Ally, pulls her in for a hug and gives her a kiss on the top of her head. "Call me or Evie if you need anything."

She gives him a small smile. "Thanks for coming."

"Anything for you, doll."

It's just me, Trevor, and Ally left in the room now. Trevor and I are still standing in the middle of the room, and it's awkward now that no one is speaking. Ally is still sitting, staring down at the water bottle in her hands.

"Well, I guess I'll let you two talk," Trevor finally says. Ally looks up quickly, hopefully surprised that he's leaving us alone together and not afraid. "Yell if you need me," he tells her. He gives me a nod and leaves the room.

I'm suddenly so nervous I can't stay still.

After a minute or so of silence, I sit on the sofa across from Ally. "I'm really sorry, Ally. I didn't want it to come out like that. I didn't want it to come out at all. I really meant what I said before, that I figured you'd find your way back eventually either because you remembered or because you felt it again. I really don't want you to feel pressured or anything. And I sure don't want you to feel awkward around me either."

"It's not your fault, Chase. I asked for this. I knew it might be something pretty epic." Her voice is completely devoid of feelings.

"What we had was pretty epic," I say quietly.

She looks up and meets my eyes. I finally see there are tears in hers, and it breaks my heart all over again. "You lied to me, Chase. I straight up asked you if you knew anything about that time, and you lied. I was feeling it. The pull between us. I was feeling it, and you could have just put me out of my misery then. Instead all of this happened," she raises her hands and gestures to the room, to the events that just unfolded. "And to hear all that," she continues, shaking her head in apparent disbelief, "about our entire relationship in front of my family? I just don't know what to do with all this right now. I don't know. I didn't expect this. I expected something, but not this."

And now I know just how bad I fucked up. Real bad.

"I'm sorry. I know I've said that a million times, but only because it's true. I didn't want to hurt you, Ally. I made some bad choices, thinking they were what was best for you."

"Yeah, well, I need time to think." She isn't making eye contact with me now. She's looking anywhere but in my eyes. I can feel the recently mended pieces of my heart cracking and falling apart again.

"Of course," I nod, hopeful because she didn't completely dismiss me. That's got to count for something, right? "You know where to find me if you want to talk or whatever. I'm always going to be here for you, baby girl. No matter what happens between us."

She nods absently as she stares down at the floor. I know I need to leave, and I stand up to do just that, but I'm terrified she'll never let me this close to her again. Before I can convince myself what a terrible idea it is, I step in front of her and lean forward to quickly kiss her head. Then I turn and leave the room before I can see her reaction to my kiss.

I go up to my apartment and lay back on my bed, staring at the ceiling. I should have told Ally the truth when we spent that first afternoon watching TV together. I should have told her the first time we hung out together, or when we watched the movie, before we kissed. There had been a hundred times when I should have told her about us.

But I didn't.

And now I have to live with whatever happens next.

# Epilogue
# Ally

*Two and a half years later.*

I've had a headache ever since I sat down in the auditorium for the ceremony. There's a sea of white around me. Instead of the traditional cap and gown graduation attire, we're wearing black pants or skirts with white chef coats, and tall white chef hats. Maybe it's the blinding white color scheme, in conjunction with the bright lighting. I don't know, all I know is that the four ibuprofen I popped before joining my class in the reserved seating area are not doing a thing.

There are only about seventy-five people in my graduating class, so the ceremony doesn't last too long. I can't see into the audience, but I certainly hear Alex's whoops as my name is called, and I walk across the stage. We've come a long way, my brothers and I. I haven't regained any memories since waking up from the coma, but my brothers and friends have filled my life since then with new memories.

Things were rough after the big reveal with Chase and it took some time for Alex to forgive us. It wasn't until about two months later, when they were getting ready to leave for their second six-month tour, and I was staying behind.


*They all look pained to be leaving me behind, even Joey and Evie, but I was adamant about not disrupting my schooling. I even got an apartment closer to the school, so I wouldn't have to stay in the big house all by myself and have to worry about a commute since I still wasn't driving. Knowing I'd made a few friends in class, they reluctantly agreed to the arrangement since I wouldn't be completely alone without them in town.*

*They all board the bus after hugging me goodbye. Everyone except for Alex, he didn't even say goodbye. As he walks up the bus steps and begins to disappear around the corner, I feel the walls closing in on me. I haven't had an anxiety attack in a while, but I still recognize that this feels different. This feels like my heart is being ripped from my chest.*

"Alex!" I call out, running to the bus door. Tears are streaming down my face. "Please, d-don't be mad at me anymore," I cry. I trip on the asphalt of the parking lot and collapse into myself, sobbing so hard I can't catch my breath.

Strong arms wrap around me, and I am pulled against his chest. I can sense it is Alex, my other half, twintuition, as he so often calls it. "I'm sorry, Al, I'm so damn sorry."

I wrap my arms around him and hold him tight, so tight. "I'm sorry I lied to you. I don't know why I did it, but I'm so sorry." He pulls back and lifts my face up to his. I cry harder seeing the matching tears on his face.

"Don't be sorry. I'm the one who's sorry; I was hurt, and I was acting like a jerk. I shouldn't have taken it out on you. You didn't know."

I rest my head on his chest, "I've missed you."

"I've missed you, too."

"I'm going to miss you while you're gone."

"Please. We're going to be Skyping so much that you're going to be sick of me."

I giggle at his dorkiness. "Promise me you'll be nice to him," I say quietly. He pulls back and looks at me; he knows exactly who I am talking about. "Please, Alex. It's as much *my fault as it is his, and if you forgive me, you have to forgive him, too."*

*"Ally," he sighs.*

*"No, Alex. Please," I beg. "You're going to be on that bus with him for six months. You can't be angry with him while you're on tour. You guys need to get along. If you don't, I will worry about you the whole time you're gone."*

*Alex looks over towards the bus, where everyone is now standing, watching our exchange. He sighs again, "Fine. For you, I will. I promise."*

*I hug him again. "Thank you. I love you," I tell him, and I feel him tense up. I haven't told him or Trevor that I love them since the coma. It isn't that I don't know how I feel; it didn't take me long to love them as brothers. There was just never a natural moment to say it. Right now, it feels natural. It feels true.*

*"I love you, too, Ally." He squeezes me tight and then helps me up from the ground. "You okay?" he asks, gesturing to my knees from when I fell.*

*"Yeah, I'm okay." I sniffle. My jeans protected my knees from the fall so I'm not cut up.*

*Now I want them to leave even less; I feel like Alex and I have wasted so much time with him being angry at me.*

"We'll be back real soon," he says as he leans forward and kisses my forehead.

"I know," I nod.

Trevor walks over and gives me a hug, "You okay?"

"Yeah," I smile as I hug him close. "I love you, Trev." I feel his breath catch as he reacts to my declaration.

"Love you, too, kid." His voice catches, but he still smiles as he pulls away. "See you in a few weeks in Raleigh," he calls out as he walks back to the bus.

I'm meeting them on their tour stop in Raleigh; it's close and it coincides with a short break I have from school.

"I'll see you then," I say. I go to wave to Alex and smile as I see him and Chase shake hands and share a quick bro-hug, Alex's term, not mine. Looking past Alex's shoulder, Chase catches me watching them and winks. I smile back at him.

Things between Chase and I came to a complete halt after that day at the house when he revealed everything. He apologized to me endlessly for lying, and for withholding information from me. Determined to start off with an even cleaner slate, a few days after the big reveal, I convinced him that we should 'fess up to my brothers about our more recent feelings. He agreed. They took it about as well as could be expected. Not like anything could have gotten any worse, and we were no longer acting on it. So there's that.

Chase never pressured me or tried to get me to remember what we once had. He was always there as a friend, but even that was a little strained since he so obviously loved me, and I was clearly attracted to him physically and maybe just a little more. Okay, a lot more. But I decided to focus on finishing my education since I was having a hard time with the idea of letting him back in in that way. I didn't think he would lie to me again, but I had to protect myself.

After I accept my diploma from the dean, I turn to walk off stage and startle briefly when a flash of Alex's grinning face pops into my head. That was weird. My mind clears and I hear Alex's cheers again. I look out to the crowd. I'm unable to locate him, but I smile and wave anyway. I'm finally a college graduate!

It took a little longer than planned for me to complete my programs at the Art Institute. I was working on two programs – traditional chef's school and baking. But I also took some time off to join the band on their second tour. Actually, it was their third tour, but the second one I was actually around for. I joined them for a short while, only missing one semester, but it still resulted in my taking longer to complete the programs. My school friends were so jealous, but I sent them tons of pictures. I was a little disappointed I wouldn't be graduating with them, but we still see each other often, and I know they are here today somewhere.

I wouldn't trade it for the world though, because I had a great time with them on tour. Alex and Joey were an absolute riot. And I had a great time with Evie and little Max. Max, who is now just over two years old, got into everything and says everything. He's his father's son for sure. Alex and Joey need to watch their mouths around that little man.

I meet them all in the back of the auditorium after the ceremony concludes. I can't help but smile and laugh as I'm passed from person to person for hugs and congratulations. Lucy is here from California, too. It's nice having everyone together. My school friends, Suzy, John, and Tim, fit in real well with our group, too, which is a relief for me since I won't have separate school and work lives now that I've graduated.

As usual, Chase is the last to hug me. When he pulls away, he looks down at my wrist and touches the bracelet I put on this morning. The one he apparently gave me.

"You wore it?" he asks.

I nod. Regardless of what happened between us, he still gives me butterflies and I don't quite trust my voice at the moment.

"I love it," I finally say to him. "And it seemed appropriate."

He smiles bright and nods. "It is."

To any onlookers, we probably look like a happy couple of people just talking about the day. But on the inside, I know Chase and I are still struggling. I'm struggling with not knowing what I want and if I'm ready to trust him and let him in. And he's just struggling-- without me.

Thankfully, Trevor steps over and breaks the awkwardness. "You ready?"

"Yes, let's go," I say.

We're going to Lombardi's for dinner, an Italian restaurant that I've been told was my favorite restaurant before the accident. After eating there a few times over the past couple of years, I can see why. The food is delicious and the atmosphere is so inviting. If I ever decide to open up my own restaurant, I want it to be just like Lombardi's.

The eleven of us are seated at a large table in the back, enjoying the food and wine. The guys garner some attention since their band is even bigger now, but most of the patrons are locals and give us our space.

My headache has lessened with the ibuprofen I took earlier, but it is starting to come back with a vengeance now. I try to discretely rub my temples, but Lucy, who is sitting beside me, notices and nudges me with her elbow.

"You okay?"

"Just a headache," I say quietly, but not quietly enough.

"You have a headache?" Alex asks, causing the entire table to go silent and look my way.

I roll my eyes, which it actually hurts to do, and sigh. "It's not a big deal, probably from all the excitement and the wine," I say. Something I learned early on after the coma is that when you're recovering from a brain injury and you mention the word "headache," people have the tendency to freak out. Even years later, as I'm learning. I had been hoping to keep this on the down low.

"You sure?" Trevor asks.

"Yes," I assure him. "I'm just going to go to the restroom, splash some water on my face, and take some ibuprofen." I stand from the table and Alex stands with me. "It's okay, Alex. I'm fine. I'll be right back." I smile, and he sits back down, still looking slightly worried.

I make my way to the hallway that leads to the restrooms and once I'm around the corner, a sharp pain in my head brings me to my knees. I close my eyes tight and bring my hands up to my temples, rubbing and trying to soothe the ache. The pain is absolutely blinding, but just as soon as it started, it's gone.

I lift my head up and look around, realizing where I am. I'm on the floor in the hallway for the restrooms. I don't even want to think about what could be on this floor, but I'm too stunned by what just happened to do anything about it and suddenly so exhausted. I adjust myself so that I'm sitting, with my back leaning against the wall. I pull my knees up to my chest, mindful to not flash anyone since I'm still in a skirt. I rest my head on my knees and close my eyes.

I'm not sure how long I'm on the ground before I start hearing voices, then hands on my back and shoulders. "Ally!" It's Alex. "Ally, are you okay? Dammit, I knew it wasn't just a headache!"

I pick my head up quickly, making myself a little dizzy with the sudden motion. "I'm fine, Alex."

"You're not fine! You're sitting on the dirty floor of a restaurant. Do you have any idea what might be on these floors?" I laugh since I had that same thought just a short while ago. He narrows his eyes at me, "It's not funny."

"It's kind of funny," I shrug.

"I can't believe you're being so nonchalant about this, Ally."

"I can't believe you're being so serious about this, Alex," I say, matching his tone.

He looks at me strangely. "Did you hit your head or something?"

I shake my head, "No."

"Come on," he says standing up. "Everyone is wondering where you are. You were gone a while."

"Why didn't Mom come back to get me? Why'd she send you? What if I was in the bathroom? You can't go in the ladies' room, Alex." Alex is staring at me as I stand up with a look on his face I can't define. "What?"

"You just asked about Mom," he says quietly.

"Yeah, so?" I ask, then I freeze and my eyes widen. Mom's dead. I *know* this. Then why do I feel like she's here with us? "I don't know why I said that," I tell him, my eyes filling with tears. I suddenly feel so sad. It's like I'm mourning my mother's death for the very first time. And Dad. Oh no, my daddy is dead, too. My eyes overflow, and the tears spill out, I move forward and fall into Alex's arms.

"They're gone," I cry. Alex is frozen; he hasn't even made a move to put his arms around me yet.

"What's going on?" I hear Trevor ask from behind Alex.

"I don't know," Alex whispers. "She remembers Mom and Dad, I think."

"Ally?" Trevor prompts.

I pull away from a still frozen Alex and look to Trevor, my lower lip quivering. "I want my mom and dad," I say on a sob.

His eyes widen, and he steps around Alex and pulls me in his arms. "Shh, it's okay, Ally," he says soothingly. He rubs my back as I cry. "What do you remember, sweetheart?"

What do I remember? I wonder what he means for about half a second before the realization hits that I had lost my memory. The accident that killed my mom and dad took my memory from me as well.

What do I remember?

I remember that day, graduation and dinner here at Lombardi's.

I remember my family, my brothers and my parents.

I remember high school and grade school.

I remember Lucy and Blake.

I remember the band.

I remember being in the car and seeing the headlights coming at us, too fast, too close.

I remember Chase.

I remember everything.

"I remember everything," I tell him.

He steps back and looks at me. "Everything?" He looks past me to Alex as his eyes fill with tears. Alex steps around so he's standing beside Trevor, his eyes full of emotion as well.

I nod, "Everything." They both hug me, and I try to hug them back, as best I can considering this is an awkward three-way hug. We all eventually break apart and laugh.

"Maybe we should call Dr. Moody," Trevor suggests. "I'm sure it isn't easy remembering everything all at once. And about Mom and Dad. You should talk to her." I frown at the mention of my parents. I know Trevor is right, and I should probably talk to my shrink. I don't see her as regularly as I did, but I still go in once every two months and call as needed. "You haven't really had a chance to properly mourn."

"Later. Is that okay? Can we call her later? Tomorrow maybe? I feel okay right now, and I kind of just want to enjoy this moment and see everyone without her psychoanalyzing me."

"First thing tomorrow morning, then." Always serious, always in control, always Trevor.

"Is everything okay?" A voice asks from behind Trevor and Alex. I'd recognize that voice anywhere.

My brothers turn to face him, and as they do I catch a glimpse of him in between them and look into his sky blue eyes. I see everything in them. Our first kiss in the rain. Us lying under the stars looking up at our moon. Sharing everything with each other. Secret moments, touches, kisses. But most of all, love. I see love in his eyes, and he must see it in mine as well because he takes a cautious step towards me.

"Ally?" he asks tentatively. My brothers look between me and Chase, not knowing whether to intervene or let this play out. They probably wonder just how much I really do remember, and whether or not what Chase told us all was true that momentous day.

"Chase," I whisper as I exhale the breath I didn't realize I'd been holding. Then I smile, and he raises his eyebrows in either question or surprise, I'm not really sure. But I don't care. Because I love him, and I know by the look in his eyes, that he still loves me.

Suddenly, I don't care that he lied to me. His reasoning all makes sense. He loves me. I love him. There's no question about it. He was scared. He wanted to protect me. Suddenly it's all a no-brainer. Why had I ever doubted this man?

I don't waste another minute and launch myself at him. He wraps his arms around me and holds me tight. "God, I missed you baby girl," he says, pulling me even closer to him, if that's possible. It's like he's afraid he'll lose me again if he lets go.

"I'm not going anywhere, ever again." I assure him, holding on tighter.

After a moment he pulls back, looking into my eyes as if he's trying to determine if this is all real. "You remember." It's a statement, not a question.

"I love you," I tell him, and I watch as his eyes fill.

"I love you, too. So much. I never stopped." He kisses me and pulls me back into him and I smile. This feeling is perfect. Being with Chase is like being home.

A throat clearing close by has us finally breaking apart, but Chase takes my hand and I smile down at where we're joined. I look up at his face, and he's smiling, too. Yes, this is perfect.

"I don't mean to interrupt your little moment," Alex says. "But we're still standing in the back hallway of a restaurant." I look over to him, expecting him to be annoyed at my behavior with Chase, but he's smiling. He and Trevor both are. He nods to the dining area of the restaurant, and we all make our way out.

"Oh, I need to go wash my face! I probably look a mess from all the crying," I say, stopping my forward motion.

Chase looks at me. "You look beautiful. You always look beautiful."

I must have stars in my eyes and a big goofy grin on my face because Alex sighs and rolls his eyes. "This is going to be sooo much fun." Chase and I laugh as he pulls me back to our table.

Trevor takes my seat by Lucy so I can sit down next to Chase.

"He's right, you know," Chase says quietly into my ear. His breath so close makes me shiver.

"About what?" I ask, knowing that Alex is rarely ever right about anything.

"This is going to be sooo much fun," he smirks.

Looking into his eyes, I say, "It's going to be everything."

He smiles, leans in, and gives me a quick kiss. I lean into him, immediately wanting more, but draw back when a breadstick bounces off Chase's head.

"That's still my sister," Alex says. I look at Chase, and we laugh. "Take it down a notch," he warns, which earns laughs from the rest of the table. "What?"

"You," Joey says, "acting like a big brother."

"I *am* her big brother," he argues.

"By like four minutes," I huff.

"Still older," he grumbles.

And so it goes, Alex and I participate in our usual banter as I field questions from the rest of the group about suddenly having my memory back. All the while, Chase is holding my hand under the table, giving me his silent strength as I share the more difficult parts about remembering my parents.

I don't miss the irony of this all coming back to me at the last place my family was all together, and on another graduation night at that. In fact, in later sessions with Dr. Moody, she shares that it was possibly the almost identical recurrence of events that triggered the memories to begin with – the graduation and the dinner. I don't really care how it happened, just that it did happen and that I can finally start living my life again.

# Chase

*Six months later.*

"Is that the last of it?" Ally asks as I walk into the apartment with two more boxes.

"That's it," I tell her, setting them down in the living room. I look around her, actually, *our*, apartment and smile when I see she has begun to unpack some of my things. Seeing my things mixed with hers is a little unreal. This moment has been years in the making.

"What's got you smiling over there?" She tilts her head and smiles as she looks at me.

"This, all of this. I just can't believe how far we've come."

"I can," she says confidently. "I knew when I was seventeen that I was going to be with you for the rest of my life." I smile at her confidence. I was that confident once, too. Then the accident happened and the love of my life was lost to me for four years. "Did you ever doubt it?"

I can't lie to her, not again. Never again. "There were times over the past few years when I wasn't sure what was going to happen."

She pauses her unpacking and steps around the kitchen table to me. Resting her hand on my cheek she says, "I'm so sorry I ever made you doubt us."

I shake my head. "No, baby girl. You have nothing to apologize for. Neither of us could help what happened. What matters is that we're together now. That you found your way back to me." I lean forward and kiss her forehead.

"I love you so much, Chase Baker."

"I love you so much, future Mrs. Baker the baker."

She laughs and pats my chest. "Funny." She returns to the kitchen and finishes unpacking my minimal kitchen supplies.

What she doesn't know, is that I plan to make her Mrs. Baker the baker sooner rather than later. Her ring has been burning a hole in my pocket for six months now. Yes, the moment she came back to me, I bought the ring. I haven't decided how I'm going to ask her yet, but I will make it epic. Her brothers would kick my ass if I didn't give Ally the very best.

Things were different, to say the least, after she regained her memory. She and I were as good as we were before the accident, but her brothers found the situation so incredibly awkward. I couldn't exactly blame them. I'm sure some part of them was holding out hope that I hallucinated the depth of our relationship or our relationship entirely. But when she all but confirmed it at the restaurant after her memory came back, they couldn't hide in denial any longer. It might have been easier if they had been eased into the whole thing, but to Ally, she loved me the same as she did the night of her high school graduation. Much to her brothers' chagrin, she wasn't about to hold back.

While she was diving in head first, I *was* trying to ease into things. I loved her more and more with each passing day, but I wanted to make sure her new life meshed with her old life. I wanted to make sure her current feelings were equivalent to her recalled feelings. I didn't want to pressure her, even though I couldn't imagine life without her. She never wavered in her love for me though. And eventually her brothers stopped acting weird and accepted it for what it was.

She started asking me to move in almost immediately after her memories returned, but for the aforementioned reasons, I declined. Of course, I ended up spending more nights at her apartment than not, but that's where I drew the line. We still hadn't slept together. Yes, I'm now a twenty-six year old virgin. But if it means being with the only girl I've ever loved with my whole heart, then Ally is worth all the sexual frustration in the world.

"Babe!" I jump at her shout. She's back in the kitchen unpacking the box and I'm still standing in the living room, doing nothing. "Where'd you go?"

"Just thinking about how far we've come, baby girl."

She smiles. "We have come a long way, baby."

\*\*\*

*One week later.*

I decide I'm going to propose to Ally tonight. I spoke with Trevor and Alex earlier today at the studio, and they gave me their blessing, after giving me some grief. I pick up some champagne and roses on my way home.

"Baby girl, where are you?" I ask after I set the vase on the kitchen table and put the champagne in the fridge.

"In here." Her voice is coming from the bedroom. I walk down the short hallway and open the bedroom door. What the fuck? There are candles lit on nearly every surface of the bedroom, and rose petals on the floor and bed. Why did I not think of this? She better not be proposing to me!

"Ally?" I don't see her in the bedroom, but her voice came from here. Just then, the closet door slowly opens and my jaw drops. Ally is leaning on the doorframe, wearing nothing but a sexy, red lace nightie. I gulp. "Baby girl?"

"Hey, handsome," she smiles, obviously pleased by the fact that she's completely struck me stupid. She struts over to me, and I can't take my eyes off her perfect body with its perfect curves in all the right perfect places. She's just perfect. "What's the matter? Cat got your tongue?"

"You look beautiful," I say, and my voice comes out hoarse. She giggles in response.

"Can't say that I don't love that I have this effect on you," she smirks.

"What's going on?" I ask, running my eyes up and down her body, fisting my hands by my side to resist reaching out and touching her everywhere.

She leans towards me, pressing her upper body against my chest. "I'm ready, Chase," she whispers seductively in my ear.

"Ready?"

She nods. "For you to make love to me."

I gulp again, "Make love to you?"

She nods again. "I want you to take me, Chase."

*Holy shit.*

Before Ally and I got together years ago, I'd fooled around with some girls. Mostly over the clothes stuff, never anything serious. But damn if I don't feel like a twelve year old boy looking at his first Playboy magazine. I don't know whether to jump for joy or cry.

"Chase?"

"Hmm?"

"What do you think?"

"Think?"

"Are you going to keep repeating everything I say?" She laughs, and I snap out of it.

"Sorry, baby girl. You've caught me completely off guard. You're so damn beautiful. Perfect. You're perfect, too."

She smiles sweetly, "Thanks, baby."

"I would like nothing more than to make love to you," I say as I place my hands on her hips and pull her lower half against me, too. She smiles as she looks up at me and I can't help but kiss her. She tastes so sweet. I pull back, "but there's something I need to do first."

She looks at me in question, then her eyes widen in surprise as I get down on one knee. "Chase?"

"Allyson Monroe, I know we only fell in love a few years ago, and we've spent quite a bit of time since then apart, but I feel like I've loved you my whole life. Those years you were lost to me, I never gave up hope that one day we'd be together again, that you'd find your way back to me. And you did. Twice. I love you more than life itself, and I want to spend the rest of my life with you. I asked your brothers permission, they said yes." She smiles through the tears in her eyes.

"But there's something else I need to tell you, too," I continue. "At your high school graduation, your mom," I pause to control my emotions. It's still hard thinking about Mr. and Mrs. Monroe. "Your mom told me that she and your dad knew about us." Ally's eyes widen in surprise. "She said that they wanted you to be happy, and they could tell that I made you happy." The tears she had been trying to contain spill over and she kneels down in front of me, wrapping her arms around me. I can feel her body shaking with her tears, and I hold her and rub her back for a moment.

When she stops crying, I pull back and look into her eyes. "She said she knew I'd take good care of you, so I feel like they would have given this their blessing, too." She smiles a watery smile and nods. I reach into my pocket and pull out the ring. It's different, a perfectly round pearl set in a ring of diamonds. I picked this one out because the moment I saw it, it reminded me of the moon. Of our moon. "Allyson Marie Monroe, will you marry me?"

More tears spill as she nods enthusiastically. "Yes. Yes!"

I push the ring onto her left ring finger and pull her in for a kiss. "I love you, baby girl."

"I love you, too, Chase. So much."

"Now, no more tears," I say as I wipe her eyes. "I want to make love to my fiancée, and it would be a real hit to my ego if she's crying when it happens." She smiles and blushes, her earlier braveness obviously having dissipated some. "We don't have to," I say quickly.

"No," she shakes her head. "I want to. I'm more than ready for this. I love you so much, Chase."

"I love you, baby girl." I stand from the floor, lift her up in my arms, and carry her to the bed.

Best night of my life.


THE END.

# Acknowledgements

First, a big thanks to the readers. If you got to this page, then you took a chance on a brand new indie author and read my book. I can't tell you how much I appreciate that!

To my husband: Thank you for being patient with me while I read and write. Every. Single. Day. Thank you for encouraging me in this and in everything that I do. Thank you for your love and thank you for being my best friend.

To my family: Thank you for always supporting me, no matter what ridiculous path I choose to take. Thank you for always just being there. Thanks for being avid readers and for making books part of my life. And special thanks to my youngest-oldest sister for recommending *Hopeless* so many months ago, which ultimately led me down this path.

To my beta readers: Amanda, Lindsey, and Jules. Thank you for agreeing to take a chance read on a no-name and for providing such awesome feedback and encouragement. Thank you for enjoying my book enough to not shoot me down. Thank you for making the most horrifying experience of my life (letting someone read my book) an easy one. *Our Moon* wouldn't be what it is today without your feedback.

To Aimee: Thank you for your honesty and for giving it to me straight. Thanks for the advice and for all your hard work on the editing. Thank you for being my sounding board for nearly everything! I bet you never want to see or hear another term of endearment in your life! You are an amazing friend and I am so grateful.

To Shelley: Thank you! Thank you for loving my story and thank you giving me honest feedback. Thank you for letting me pick your brain. And thank you for being such an awesome friend!

To Sarah Robinson: Thank you for entertaining my random questions and for being so open and honest. Thank you for the advice, the pointers were so helpful. You've been like an unofficial mentor and I appreciate it so much. Thanks for reading this!

To Amanda Bianco: Thank you for not only being a beta, but for sharing advice from your own experience as a new author. Thank you for promoting me on Facebook and introducing me to so many people in the same boat. It has been so much easier to do this having someone else one step ahead of me.

To Ginni Hall: Where did you come from, girl? You have been such an unexpected surprise and one of my biggest cheerleaders! I can't thank you enough for everything you've done to promote this book and me. Thank you for believing in me and everything you've done!

You are the best PA ever and I appreciate your support more than words can say!

To Jacque Burford: Thank you for answering my Teaser Tuesday questions and for all the great advice. Bet you didn't expect to see your name here?!

To BLA: Thanks for being a bunch of awesome people who love books as much as I do. The book enthusiasm in this group is absolutely amazing and so encouraging for a baby author.

To all the readers, reviewers, and bloggers who have read, reviewed, and promoted this book: Thank you! I don't think any author could do it without your support.

To all the authors I love: Thank you for writing amazing stories and for giving me inspiration to do this myself.

To Cassy Roop of Pink Ink Designs: Lady, you are amazing. From my logo to my covers, I can say "apple" and you will turn that into exactly what I am looking for. You are so incredibly talented and I thank you so much for this cover.

# About the Author

Jennifer lives in South Carolina with her husband and their three fur-kids. She is in grad school, pursuing a Masters in Psychology for Clinical Counseling. When she is not at work or taking classes, she is either reading or writing. Books have always been a passion. She also enjoys spending time with her family, traveling to new places, and music. She released her debut novel, Our Moon, in June 2015.

# Connect With Me

Email: jenniferlallenauthor@gmail.com

Website: www.jenniferlallenauthor.com

Facebook: www.facebook.com/jallenauthor

Twitter: https://twitter.com/AuthorJenniferA

Mailing List:
https://tinyletter.com/JenniferLAllenAuthor

Goodreads:
https://www.goodreads.com/JenniferLAllen

# Books by
# Jennifer L. Allen

*Our Moon: JACT Book One*
*Hearts in the Sand: JACT Book Two*

*Change of Heart*